The Double Life of
Mr. Alfred Burton

The Double Life of Mr. Alfred Burton

E. Phillips Oppenheim

MINT EDITIONS

The Double Life of Mr. Alfred Burton was first published in 1913.

This edition published by Mint Editions 2021.

ISBN 9781513281261 | E-ISBN 9781513286280

Published by Mint Editions®

MINT
EDITIONS
minteditionsbooks.com

Publishing Director: Jennifer Newens
Design & Production: Rachel Lopez Metzger
Project Manager: Micaela Clark
Typesetting: Westchester Publishing Services

Contents

I

THE FRUIT OF THE TREE

M r. Alfred Burton, although he was blissfully and completely ignorant of the fact, stood at the door of Fate. He was a little out of breath and his silk hat was reclining at the back of his head. In his mouth was a large cigar which he felt certain was going to disagree with him, but he smoked it because it had been presented to him a few minutes ago by the client upon whom he was in attendance. He had rather deep-set blue eyes, which might have been attractive but for a certain keenness in their outlook, which was in a sense indicative of the methods and character of the young man himself; a pale, characterless face, a straggling, sandy moustache, and an earnest, not to say convincing, manner. He was dressed in such garments as the head-clerk of Messrs. Waddington & Forbes, third-rate auctioneers and house agents, might have been expected to select. He dangled a bunch of keys in his hand.

"If this house don't suit you, sir," he declared, confidently, "why, there isn't one in the whole west-end that will. That's my opinion, anyway. There's nothing in our books to compare with it for value and accommodation. We nearly let it last week to Lord Leconside, but Her Ladyship—she came round with me herself—decided that it was just a trifle too large. As a matter of fact, sir," this energetic young man went on, confidentially, "the governor insisted upon a deposit and it didn't seem to be exactly convenient. It isn't always these people with titles who've got the money. That we find out in our business, sir, as quickly as anybody. As for the steam heating you were talking about, Mr. Lynn, why, that's all very well for New York," he continued, persuasively, "but over here the climate doesn't call for it—you can take it from me that it doesn't, indeed, Mr. Lynn. I have the letting in my hands of as many houses as most people, and you can take it from me, sir, as the direct result of my experience, that over here they won't have it—won't have it at any price, sir. Most unhealthy we find it, and always produces a rare crop of colds and coughs unknown to those that are used to an honest coal fire. It's all a matter of climate, sir, after all, isn't it?"

The young man paused to take breath. His client, who had been listening attentively in gloomy but not unappreciative silence, removed his cigar from his mouth. He was a middle-aged American with a wife and daughters on their way over from New York, and his business was to take a house before they arrived. It wasn't a job he liked, but he was making the best of it. This young man appealed to his sense of business.

"Say," he remarked, approvingly, "you've learned how to talk in your trade!"

Stimulated by this encouragement, Alfred Burton clapped on his hat a little more securely, took a long breath, and went at it again.

"Why, I'm giving myself a rest this morning, sir!" he declared. "I haven't troubled to tell you more than the bare facts. This house doesn't need any talking about—doesn't need a word said about it. Her Ladyship's last words to us were—Lady Idlemay, you know, the owner of the house—'Mr. Waddington and Mr. Burton,' she said—she was speaking to us both, for the governor always introduces me to clients as being the one who does most of the letting,—'Mr. Waddington and Mr. Burton,' she said, 'if a tenant comes along whom you think I'd like to have living in my rooms and using my furniture, breathing my air, so to speak, why, go ahead and let the house, rents being shockingly low just now, with agricultural depression and what not, but sooner than not let it to gentlepeople, I'll do without the money,' Her Ladyship declared. Now you're just the sort of tenant she'd like to have here. I'm quite sure of that, Mr. Lynn. I should take a pleasure in bringing you two together."

Mr. Lynn grunted. He was perfectly well aware that the house would seem more desirable to his wife and daughters from the very fact that it belonged to a "Lady" anybody. He was perfectly well aware, also, that his companion had suspected this. The consideration of these facts left him, however, unaffected. He was disposed, if anything, to admire the cleverness of the young man who had realized an outside asset.

"Well, I've seen pretty well all over it," he remarked. "I'll go back to the office with you, anyhow, and have a word with Mr. Waddington. By the way, what's that room behind you?"

The young man glanced carelessly around at the door of the room of Fate and down at the bunch of keys which he held in his hand. He even chuckled as he replied.

"I was going to mention the matter of that room, sir," he replied, "because, if perfectly agreeable to the tenant, Her Ladyship would like to keep it locked up."

"Locked up?" Mr. Lynn repeated. "And why?"

"Regular queer story, sir," the young man declared, confidentially. "The late Earl was a great traveller in the East, as you may have heard, and he was always poking about in some ruined city or other in the desert, and picking up things and making discoveries. Well, last time he came home from abroad, he brought with him an old Egyptian or Arab,—I don't know which he was, but he was brown,—settled him down in this room—in his own house, mind—and wouldn't have him disturbed or interfered with, not at any price. Well, the old chap worked here night and day at some sort of writing, and then, naturally enough, what with not having the sort of grub he liked, and never going outside the doors, he croaked."

"He what?" Mr. Lynn interposed.

"He died," the young man explained. "It was just about the time that the Earl was ill himself. His Lordship gave orders that the body was to be buried and the room locked up, in case the old chap's heirs should come along. Seems he'd brought a few odd things of his own over— nothing whatever of any value. Anyway, those were Lord Idlemay's wishes, and the room has been locked up ever since."

Mr. Lynn was interested.

"No objection to our just looking inside, I suppose?"

"None whatever," the young man declared, promptly. "I was going to have a peep myself. Here goes!"

He fitted the key in the lock and pushed the door open. Mr. Lynn took one step forward and drew back hurriedly.

"Thanks!" he said. "That'll do! I've seen all I want—and smelt!"

Mr. Alfred Burton, fortunately or unfortunately, was possessed of less sensitive nasal organs and an indomitable curiosity. The room was dark and stuffy, and a wave of pungent odor swept out upon them with the opening of the door. Nevertheless, he did not immediately close it.

"One moment!" he muttered, peering inside. "I'll just look around and see that everything is in order."

He crossed the threshold and passed into the room. It was certainly a curious apartment. The walls were hung not with paper at all, but with rugs of some Oriental material which had the effect of still further increasing the gloom. There were neither chairs nor tables—no furniture at all, in fact, of any account but in the furthest corner was a great pile of cushions, and on the floor by the side a plain strip of sandalwood, covered with a purple cloth, on which were several square-shaped sheets of paper, a brass inkstand, and a bundle of quill pens. On the extreme corner of this strip of wood, which seemed to have been used as a writing desk by some one reclining upon the cushions, was the strangest article of all. Alfred Burton stared at it with wide-open eyes. It was a tiny plant growing out of a small-sized flower-pot, with real green leaves and a cluster of queer little brown fruit hanging down from among them.

"Jiminy!" the clerk exclaimed. "I say, Mr. Lynn, sir!"

But Mr. Lynn had gone off to pace the dining-room once more. Burton moved slowly forward and stooped down over the cushions. He took up the sheets of paper which lay upon the slab of sandalwood. They were covered with wholly indecipherable characters save for the last page only, and there, even as he stood with it in his fingers, he saw, underneath the concluding paragraph of those unintelligible hieroglyphics, a few words of faintly traced English, laboriously printed, probably a translation. He struck a match and read them slowly out to himself:

"It is finished. The nineteenth generation has triumphed. He who shall eat of the brown fruit of this tree shall see the things of Life and Death as they are. He who shall eat—" The translation concluded abruptly. Mr. Alfred Burton removed his silk hat and reflectively scratched his head.

"Queer sort of joker he must have been," he remarked to himself. "I wonder what he was getting at?"

His eyes fell upon the little tree. He felt the earth in the pot it was quite dry. Yet the tree itself was fresh and green.

"Here goes for a brown bean," he continued, and plucked one.

Even then, while he held it in his fingers, he hesitated.

"Don't suppose it will do me any harm," he muttered, doubtfully.

There was naturally no reply. Mr. Alfred Burton laughed uneasily to himself. The shadows of the room and its curious perfume were a trifle disconcerting.

"Risk it, anyway," he concluded. "Here goes!" He raised the little brown fruit—which did indeed somewhat resemble a bean—to his mouth and swallowed it. He found it quite tasteless, but the deed was no sooner done than he was startled by a curious buzzing in his ears and a momentary but peculiar lapse of memory. He sat and looked around him like a man who has been asleep and suddenly awakened in unfamiliar surroundings. Then the sound of his client's voice suddenly recalled him to himself. He started up and peered through the gloom.

"Who's there?" he asked, sharply.

"Say, young man, I am waiting for you when you're quite ready," Mr. Lynn remarked from the threshold. "Queer sort of atmosphere in there, isn't it?"

Mr. Alfred Burton came slowly out and locked the door of the room. Even then he was dimly conscious that something had happened to him. He hated the musty odor of the place, the dusty, unswept hall, and the general air of desertion. He wanted to get out into the street and he hurried his client toward the front door. As soon as he had locked up, he breathed a little sigh of relief.

"What a delicious soft wind!" he exclaimed, removing his unsightly hat. "Really, I think that when we get a sunny day like this, April is almost our most beautiful month."

Mr. Lynn stared at his companion, who was now slowly descending the steps.

"Say, about this house," he began, "I guess I'd better take it. It may not be exactly what I want but it seems to me to be about as near as anything I am likely to find. We'll go round to the office right away and fix things up."

Mr. Alfred Burton shook his head doubtfully.

"I don't think I would take it, if I were you, Mr. Lynn," he said.

Mr. Lynn stopped short upon the pavement and looked at his companion in amazement. The latter had the air of one very little interested in the subject of conversation. He was watching approvingly a barrowful of lilac and other spring flowers being wheeled along by a flower-seller in the middle of the road.

"What an exquisite perfume!" the young man murmured, enthusiastically. "Doesn't it remind you, Mr. Lynn, of a beautiful garden somewhere right away in the country—one of those old-fashioned gardens, you know, with narrow paths where you have to push your way through the flowers, and where there are always great beds of pink and white stocks near the box edges? And do you notice—an accident, of course—but what a delicate blend of color the lilac and those yellow jonquils make!"

"I can't smell anything," the American declared, a little impatiently, "and I don't know as I want to just now. I am here to talk business, if you don't mind."

"In one moment," Burton replied. "Excuse me for one moment, if you please."

He hastened across the street and returned a moment or two later with a bunch of violets in his hand. Mr. Lynn watched him, partly in amazement, partly in disapproval. There seemed to be very little left of the smart, businesslike young man whose methods, only a short time ago, had commanded his unwilling admiration. Mr. Alfred Burton's expression had undergone a complete change. His eyes had lost their calculating twinkle, his mouth had softened. A pleasant but somewhat abstracted smile had taken the place of his forced amiability.

"You will forgive me, won't you?" he said, as he regained the pavement. "I really haven't smelt violets before this year. Spring comes upon us Londoners so suddenly."

"About that house, now," the American insisted, a little sharply.

"Certainly," Burton replied, removing his eyes unwillingly from the passing barrow. "I really don't think you had better take it, Mr. Lynn. You see, it is not generally known, but there is no doubt that Lord Idlemay had typhoid fever there."

"Typhoid!" Mr. Lynn exclaimed, incredulously.

His companion nodded.

"Two of the servants were down with it as well," he continued. "We implored Lady Idlemay, when she offered us the letting of the house, to have the drains put in thorough order, but when we got the estimate out for her she absolutely declined. To tell you the truth, the best agents had all refused, under the circumstances, to have the house upon their books at all. That is why we got the letting of it."

Mr. Lynn removed the cigar from his mouth for a moment. There was a slight frown Upon his forehead. He was puzzled.

"Say, you're not getting at me for any reason, are you?" he demanded.

"My dear sir!" Burton protested, eagerly. "I am simply doing my duty and telling you the truth. The house is not in a fit state to be let to any one— certainly not to a man with a family. If you will permit me to say so, you are not going the right way to secure a suitable house. You simply walked into our office because you saw the sign up, and listened to anything the governor had to say. We haven't any west-end houses at all upon our books. It isn't our business, unfortunately. Miller & Sons, or Roscoe's, are the best people. No one would even come to see you at Idlemay House, much less stay with you—the place has such a bad reputation."

"Then will you be good enough to just explain to me why you were cracking it up like blazes only a few minutes ago?" Mr. Lynn demanded, indignantly. "I nearly took the darned place!"

Mr. Burton shook his head penitently.

"I am afraid that I cannot explain, sir," he confessed. "To tell you the truth, I do not understand in the least how I could have brought myself to be so untruthful. I am only thankful that no harm has been done."

They had reached the corner of the street in which the offices of Messrs. Waddington & Forbes were situated. Mr. Lynn came to a full stop.

"I can't see but what we might just as well part here, young man," he declared. "There's no use in my coming to your office, after what you've told me."

"Not the slightest," Mr. Burton admitted frankly, "in fact you are better away. Mr. Waddington would certainly try to persuade you to take the house. If you'll accept my advice, sir, you will go to Miller & Sons in St. James's Place. They have all the best houses on their books and they are almost certain to find something to suit you."

Mr. Lynn gazed once more at his companion curiously.

"Say, I'm not quite sure that I can size you up, even now," he said. "At first I thought that you were a rare little hustler, right on the job. I was set against that house and yet you almost persuaded me into taking it. What's come over you, anyway?"

Mr. Burton shook his head dubiously.

"I am afraid that it is no use asking me," he replied, "for I really don't quite know myself."

Mr. Lynn still lingered. The longer he looked at his companion, the more he appreciated the subtle change of demeanor and language which had certainly transformed Mr. Alfred Burton.

"It was after you came out of that little room," he continued, meditatively, "where that Oriental fellow had been shut up. The more I think of it, the odder it seems. You were as perky as mustard when you went in and you've been sort of dazed ever Since you came out."

Mr. Burton lifted his hat.

"Good day, sir!" he said. "I trust that you will find a residence to suit you."

Mr. Lynn strolled off with a puzzled frown upon his forehead, and Alfred Burton, with a slight gesture of aversion, pushed open the swinging doors which led into the offices of Messrs. Waddington & Forbes.

II

A Transformation

Burton stood for a moment upon the threshold of the office, looking around him. A new and peculiar distaste for these familiar surroundings seemed suddenly to have sprung into life. For the first time he realized the intense ugliness of this scene of his daily labors. The long desk, ink-splashed and decrepit, was covered with untidy piles of papers, some of them thick with dust; the walls were hung with seedy-looking files and an array of tattered bills; there were cobwebs in every corner, gaps in the linoleum floor-covering. In front of the office-boy—a youth about fourteen years of age, who represented the remaining clerical staff of the establishment—were pinned up several illustrations cut out from *Comic Cuts*, the *Police News*, and various other publications of a similar order. As Burton looked around him, his distaste grew. It seemed impossible that he had ever existed for an hour amid such an environment. The prospect of the future was suddenly hugely distasteful.

Very slowly he changed his coat and climbed on to his worn horsehair stool, without exchanging his usual facetious badinage with the remaining member of the staff. The office-boy, who had thought of something good to say, rather resented his silence. It forced him into taking the initiative, a position which placed him from the first at a disadvantage.

"Any luck with the Yank, Mr. Burton?" he inquired, with anxious civility.

Burton shook his head.

"None at all," he confessed. "He wouldn't have anything to do with the house."

"Has any one been letting on to him about it, do you think?"

"I don't think so," Burton replied. "I don't think any one else has mentioned it to him at all. He seems to be a complete stranger here."

"Couldn't have been quite at your best, could you, Mr. Burton, sir? Not your usual bright and eloquent self, eh?"

The boy grinned and then ducked, expecting a missile. None came, however. Alfred Burton was in a very puzzled state of mind, and he neither showed nor indeed felt any resentment. He turned and faced his subordinate.

"I really don't know, Clarkson," he admitted. "I am sure that I was quite polite, and I showed him everything he wished to see; but, of course, I had to tell him the truth about the place."

"The what?" young Clarkson inquired, in a mystified tone.

"The truth," Burton repeated.

"Wot yer mean?"

"About the typhoid and that," Burton explained, mildly.

The office-boy pondered for a moment. Then he slowly opened a ledger, drew a day-book towards him, and continued his work. He was being jollied, of course, but the thing was too subtle for him at present. He decided to wait for the next move. Burton continued to regard his subordinate, however, and by degrees an expression of pained disapproval crept into his face.

"Clarkson," he said, "if you will forgive my mentioning a purely personal matter, why do you wear such uncomfortable collars and such an exceedingly unbecoming tie?"

The office-boy swung round upon his stool. His mouth was wide open like a rabbit's. He fingered the offending articles.

"What's the matter with them?" he demanded, getting his question out with a single breath.

"Your collars are much too high," Burton pointed out. "One can see how they cut into your neck. Then why wear a tie of that particular shade of vivid purple when your clothes themselves, with that blue and yellow stripe, are somewhat noticeable? There is a lack of symphony about the arrangement, an entire absence of taste, which is apt to depress one. The whole effect which you produce upon one's vision is abominable. You won't think my mentioning this a liberty, I hope?"

"What about your own red tie and dirty collar?" young Clarkson asked, indignantly. "What price your eight and sixpenny trousers, eh, with the blue stripe and the grease stains? What about the sham diamond stud in your dickey, and your three inches of pinned on cuff? Fancy your appearance, perhaps! Why, I wouldn't walk the streets in such a rig-out!"

Burton listened to his junior's attack unresentingly but with increasing bewilderment. Then he slipped from his seat and walked hurriedly across to the looking-glass, which he took down from its nail. He gazed at himself long and steadily and from every possible angle. It is probable that for the first time in his life he saw himself then as he really was. He was plain, of insignificant appearance, he was ill and tastelessly dressed. He stood there before the sixpenny-ha'penny mirror and drank the cup of humiliation.

"Calling my tie, indeed!" the office-boy muttered, his smouldering resentment bringing him back to the attack. "Present from my best girl, that was, and she knows what's what. Young lady with a place in a west-end milliner's shop, too. If that doesn't mean good taste, I should like to know what does. Look at your socks, too, all coming down over the tops of your boots! Nasty dirty pink and green stripes! There's another thing about my collar, too," he continued, speaking with renewed earnestness as he appreciated his senior's stupefaction. "It was clean yesterday, and that's more than yours was—or the day before!"

Burton shivered as he finally turned away from that looking-glass. The expression upon his face was indescribable.

"I am sorry I spoke, Clarkson," he apologized humbly. "It certainly seemed to have slipped my memory that I myself—I can't think how I managed to make such hideous, unforgivable mistakes."

"While we are upon the subject," his subordinate continued, ruthlessly, "why don't you give your fingernails a scrub sometimes, eh? You might give your coat a brush, too, now and then, while you are about it. All covered with scurf and dust about the shoulders! I'm all for cleanliness, I am."

Burton made no reply. He was down and his junior kicked him.

"I'd like to see the color of your shirt if you took those paper cuffs off!" the latter exclaimed. "Why don't you chuck that rotten dickey away? Cave!"

The door leading into the private office was brusquely opened. Mr. Waddington, the only existing member of the firm, entered—a large, untidy-looking man, also dressed in most uncomely fashion, and wearing an ill-brushed silk hat on the back of his head. He turned at once to his righthand man.

"Well, did you land him?" he demanded, with some eagerness.

Burton shook his head regretfully.

"It was quite impossible to interest him in the house at all, sir," he declared. "He seemed inclined to take it at first, but directly he understood the situation he would have nothing more to do with it."

Mr. Waddington's face fell. He was disappointed. He was also puzzled.

"Understood the situation," he repeated. "What the dickens do you mean, Burton? What situation?"

"I mean about the typhoid, sir, and Lady Idlemay's refusal to have the drains put in order."

Mr. Waddington's expression for a few moments was an interesting and instructive study. His jaw had fallen, but he was still too bewildered to realize the situation properly.

"But who told him?" he gasped.

"I did," Burton replied gently. "I could not possibly let him remain in ignorance of the facts."

"You couldn't—what?"

"I could not let him the house without explaining all the circumstances, sir," Burton declared, watching his senior anxiously. "I am sure you would not have wished me to do anything of the sort, would you?"

What Mr. Waddington said was unimportant. There was very little that he forgot and he was an auctioneer with a low-class clientele and a fine flow of language. When he had finished, the office-boy was dumb with admiration. Burton was looking a little pained and he had the shocked expression of a musician who has been listening to a series of discords. Otherwise he was unmoved.

"Your duty was to let that house," Mr. Waddington wound up, striking the palm of one hand with the fist of the other. "What do I give you forty-four shillings a week for, I should like to know? To go and blab trade secrets to every customer that comes along? If you couldn't get him to sign the lease, you ought to have worked a deposit, at any rate. He'd have had to forfeit that, even if he'd found out afterwards."

"I am sorry," Burton said, speaking in a much lower tone than was usual with him, but with a curious amount of confidence. "It would have been a moral falsehood if I had attempted anything of the sort. I could not possibly offer the house to Mr. Lynn or anybody else, without disclosing its drawbacks."

The auctioneer's face had become redder. His eyes seemed on the point of coming out of his head. He became almost incoherent.

"God bless my soul!" he spluttered. "Have you gone mad, Burton? What's come to you since the morning? Have you changed into a blithering fool, or what?"

"I think not, sir," Burton replied, gravely. "I don't—exactly remember for the moment," he went on with a slight frown. "My head seems a little confused, but I cannot believe that it has been our custom to conduct our business in the fashion you are suggesting."

Mr. Waddington walked round the office, holding his head between his hands.

"I don't suppose either of us has been drinking at this hour in the morning," he muttered, when he came to a standstill once more. "Look here, Burton, I don't want to do anything rash. Go home—never mind the time—go home this minute before I break out again. Come to-morrow morning, as usual. We'll talk it out then. God bless my soul!" he added, as Burton picked up his hat with a little sigh of relief and turned toward the door. "Either I'm drunk or the fellow's got religion or something! I never heard such infernal rubbish in my life!"

"Made a nasty remark about my tie just now, sir," Clarkson said, with dignity, as his senior disappeared. "Quite uncalled for. I don't fancy he can be well."

"Ever known him like it before?" Mr. Waddington inquired.

"Never, sir. I thought he seemed chippier than ever this morning when he went out. His last words were that he'd bet me a packet of Woodbines that he landed the old fool."

"He's gone dotty!" the auctioneer decided, as he turned back towards his sanctum. "He's either gone dotty or he's been drinking. The last chap in the world I should have thought it of!"

THE MENTAL ATTITUDE OF ALFRED BURTON, as he emerged into the street, was in some respects curious. He was not in the least sorry for what had happened. On the contrary, he found himself wishing that the day's respite had not been granted to him, and that his departure from the place of his employment was final. He was very much in the position of a man who has been transferred without warning or notice from the streets of London to the streets of Pekin. Every object which he saw he looked upon with different eyes. Every face which he passed produced a different impression upon him. He looked about him with all the avidity of one suddenly conscious of a great store of unused impressions. It was like a second birth. He neither understood the situation nor attempted to analyze it. He was simply conscious of a most delightful and inexplicable light-heartedness, and of a host of sensations which seemed to produce at every moment some new pleasure. His first and most pressing anxiety was a singular one. He loathed himself from head to foot. He shuddered as he passed the shop-windows for fear he should see his own reflection. He made his way unfalteringly to an outfitter's shop, and from there, with a bundle under his arm, to the baths. It was a very different Alfred Burton indeed who, an hour or two later, issued forth into the streets. Gone was the Cockney young man with the sandy moustache, the cheap silk hat worn at various angles to give himself a rakish air, the flashy clothes, cheap and pretentious, the assured, not to say bumptious air so sedulously copied from the deportment of his employer. Enter a new and completely transformed Alfred Burton, an inoffensive-looking young man in a neat gray suit, a lilac-colored tie of delicate shade, a flannel shirt with no pretence at cuffs, but with a spotless turned down collar, a soft Homburg hat, a clean-shaven lip. With a new sense of self-respect and an immense feeling of relief, Burton, after a few moments' hesitation, directed his footsteps towards the National Gallery. He had once been there years ago on a wet Bank Holiday, and some faint instinct of memory which somehow or other had survived the burden of his sordid days suddenly reasserted itself. He climbed the steps and passed through the portals with the beating heart of the explorer who climbs his last hill. It was his entrance, this, into the new world whose call was tearing at his heartstrings. He bought no catalogue, he asked no questions. From room to room he passed with untiring footsteps. His whole being was filled with the immeasurable relief, the almost passionate joy, of one who for the first time is able to gratify a new and marvelous appetite. With his eyes, his soul, all these late-born, strange, appreciative powers, he ministered to an appetite which seemed unquenchable. It was dusk when he came out, his cheeks burning, his eyes bright. He carried a new music, a whole world of new joys with him, but his most vital sensation was one of glowing and passionate sympathy. They were splendid, these heroes who had seen the truth and had struggled to give life to it with pencil or brush or chisel, that others, too, might see and understand. If only one could do one's little share!

He walked slowly along, absorbed in his thoughts, unconscious even of the direction in which his footsteps were taking him. When at last he paused, he was outside a theatre. The name of Ibsen occupied a prominent place upon the boards. From somewhere among the hidden cells of his memory came a glimmering recollection—a word or two read at random, an impression, only half understood, yet the germ of which had survived. Ibsen! A prophet of truth, surely! He looked eagerly down the placard for the announcements and the prices of admission. And then a sudden cold douche of memory descended upon his new enthusiasms. There was Ellen!

III

Mr. Alfred Burton's Family

There certainly was Ellen! Like a man on his way to prison, Alfred Burton took his place in a third-class carriage in his customary train to Garden Green. Ned Miles, who travelled in the oil trade, came up and smote him upon the shoulder.

"Say, cocky, what have you been doing to yourself?" he demanded in amazement. "Have you robbed a bank and going about in disguise, eh? Why, the missis won't know you!"

Burton shrank a little back in his place. His eyes seemed filled with some nameless distaste as he returned the other's gaze.

"I have taken a dislike to my former style of dress," he replied simply, "also to my moustache."

"Taken a dislike—Lord love a duck!" his quondam friend exclaimed. "Strike me blind if I should have known you! Taken a dislike to the— here, Alf, is this a game?"

"Not at all," Burton answered quietly. "It is the truth. It is one of those matters, I suppose," he continued, "which principally concern oneself."

"No need to get jumpy about it," Mr. Miles remarked, still a little dazed. "Come in and have some farthing nap with the boys. They won't recognize you in that get-up. We'll have a lark with them."

Burton shook his head. Again he was unable to keep the distaste from his eyes or tone.

"Not to-night, thank you."

The train was just moving, so Miles was obliged to hurry off, but at Garden Green, Burton was compelled to run the gauntlet of their cheers and mockery as he passed down the platform. Good sports and excellent fellows he had thought them yesterday. To-day he had no words for them. He simply knew that they grated upon every nerve in his body and that he loathed them. For the first time he began to be frightened. What was this thing that had happened to him? How was it possible for him to continue his daily life?

As soon as he was out of the station, his troubles began again. A veil seemed to have been torn from before his eyes. Just as in London every face into which he had looked, every building which he had passed, had seemed to him unfamiliar, appealing to an altered system of impressions, so here, during that brief walk, a new disgust was born in him. The showy-looking main street with its gingerbread buildings, all new and glittering with paint, appalled him. The larger villas—self-conscious types all reeking with plaster and false decorations—set him shivering. He turned into his own street and his heart sank. Something had indeed touched his eyes and he saw new and terrible things. The row of houses looked as though they had come out of a child's playbox. They were all untrue, shoddy, uninviting. The waste space on the other side of the unmade street, a repository for all the rubbish of the neighborhood, brought a groan to his lips. He stopped before the gate of his own little dwelling. There were yellow curtains in the window, tied back with red velvet. Even with the latch of the gate in his hand, he hesitated. A child in a spotted velveteen suit and a soiled lace collar, who had been playing in the street, greeted him with an amazed shout and then ran on ahead.

"Mummy, come and look at Daddy!" the boy shrieked. "He's cut off all the hair from his lip and he's got such funny clothes on! Do come and look at his hat!"

The child was puny, unprepossessing, and dirty. Worse tragedy than this, Burton knew it. The woman who presently appeared to gaze at him with open-mouthed wonder, was pretentiously and untidily dressed, with some measure of good looks woefully obscured by a hard and unsympathetic expression. Burton knew these things also. It flashed into his mind as he stood there that her first attraction to him had been because she resembled his ill-conceived idea of an actress. As a matter of fact, she resembled much more closely her cousin, who was a barmaid. Burton looked into the tragedy of his life and shivered.

"What in the name of wonder's the meaning of this, Alfred?" his better half demanded. "What are you standing there for, looking all struck of a heap?"

He made no reply. Speech, for the moment, was absolutely impossible. She stood and stared at him, her arms akimbo, disapproval written in her face. Her hair was exceedingly untidy and there was a smut upon her cheek. A soiled lace collar, fastened with an imitation diamond brooch, had burst asunder.

"What's come to your moustache?" she demanded, "And why are you dressed like—like a house-painter on a Sunday?"

Burton found his first gleam of consolation. A newly-discovered sense of humor soothed him inexplicably.

"Sorry you don't like my clothes," he replied. "You'll get used to them."

"Get used to them!" his better half repeated, almost hysterically. "Do you mean to say you are going about like that?"

"Something like it," Burton admitted.

"No silk hat, no tail coat?"

Burton shook his head gently.

"I trust," he said, "that I have finished, for the present, at any rate, with those most unsightly garments."

"Come inside," Ellen ordered briskly.

They passed into the little sitting-room. Burton glanced around him with a half-frightened sense of apprehension. His memory, at any rate, had not played him false. Everything was as bad—even worse than he had imagined. The suite of furniture which was the joy of his wife's heart had been, it is true, exceedingly cheap, but the stamped magenta velvet was as crude in its coloring as his own discarded tie. He looked at the fringed cloth upon the table, the framed oleographs upon the wall, and he was absolutely compelled to close his eyes. There was not a single thing anywhere which was not discordant.

Mrs. Burton had not yet finished with the subject of clothes. The distaste upon her face had rather increased. She looked her husband up and down and her eyes grew bright with anger.

"Well, I did think," she declared, vigorously, "that I was marrying a man who looked like a gentleman, at least! Do you mean to say, Alfred, that you mean to go into the city like that?"

"Certainly," Burton replied. "And Ellen!"

"Well?"

"Since we are upon the subject of dress, may I have a few words? You have given expression to your dislikes quite freely. You will not mind if I do the same?"

"Well, what have you got to say?" she demanded, belligerently.

"I don't like your bun," Burton said firmly.

"Don't like my what?" his wife shrieked, her hands flying to the back of her head.

"I don't like your bun—false hair, or whatever you call it," Burton repeated. "I don't like that brooch with the false diamonds, and if you can't afford a clean white blouse, I'd wear a colored one."

Mrs. Burton's mouth was open but for the moment she failed to express herself adequately. Her husband continued.

"Your skirt is fashionable, I suppose, because it is very short and very tight, but it makes you walk like a duck, and it leaves unconcealed so much of your stockings that I think at least you should be sure that they are free from holes."

"You called my skirt smart only yesterday," Ellen gasped, "and I wasn't going out of doors in these stockings."

"It is just as bad to wear them indoors or outdoors, whether any one sees them or whether any one does not," Burton insisted. "Your own sense of self-respect should tell you that. Did you happen, by the bye, to glance at the boy's collar when you put it on?"

"What, little Alf now?" his mother faltered. "You're getting on to him now, are you?"

"I certainly should wish," Burton protested mildly, "that he was more suitably dressed. A plain sailor-suit, or a tweed knickerbocker suit with a flannel collar, would be better than those velveteen things with that lace abomination. And why is he tugging at your skirt so?"

"He is ready to start," Ellen replied sharply. "Haven't forgotten you're taking us to the band, have you?"

"I had forgotten it," Burton admitted, "but I am quite willing to go."

Ellen turned towards the stairs.

"Down in five minutes," she announced. "I hope you've finished all that rubbishing talk. There's some tea in the tea-pot on the hob, if you want any. Don't upset things."

Burton drifted mechanically into the kitchen, noting its disorder with a new disapproval. He sat on the edge of the table for a few moments, gazing helplessly about him. Presently Ellen descended the stairs and called to him. He took up his hat and followed his wife and the boy out of the house. The latter eyed him wonderingly.

"Look at pa's hat!" he shouted. "Oh, my!"

Ellen stopped short upon her way to the gate.

"Alfred," she exclaimed, "you don't mean to say you're coming out with us like that—coming to the band, too, where we shall meet everyone?"

"Certainly, my dear," Burton replied, placing the object of their remarks fearlessly upon his head. "You may not be quite used to it yet, but I can assure you that it is far more becoming and suitable than a cheap silk hat, especially for an occasion like the present."

Ellen opened her mouth and closed it again—it was perhaps wise!

"Come on," she said abruptly. "Alfred wants to hear the soldier music and we are late already. Take your father's hand."

They started upon their pilgrimage. Burton, at any rate, spent a miserable two hours. He hated the stiff, brand-new public garden in which they walked, with its stunted trees, its burnt grass, its artificial and weary flower-beds. He hated the people who stood about as they did, listening to the band,—the giggling girls, the callow, cigarette-smoking youths, the dressed up, unnatural replicas of his own wife and himself, with whom he was occasionally forced to hold futile conversation. He hated the sly punch in the ribs from one of his quondam companions, the artful murmur about getting the missis to look another way and the hurried visit to a neighboring public-house, the affected anger and consequent jokes which followed upon their return. As they walked homeward, the cold ugliness of it all seemed almost to paralyze his newly awakened senses. It was their social evening of the week, looked forward to always by his wife, spoken of cheerfully by him even last night, an evening when he might have had to bring home friends to supper, to share a tin of sardines, a fragment of mutton, Dutch cheese, and beer which he himself would have had to fetch from the nearest public-house. He wiped his forehead and found that it was wet. Then Ellen broke the silence.

"What I should like to know, Alfred, is—what's come to you?" she commenced indignantly. "Not a word have you spoken all the evening—you that there's no holding generally with your chaff and jokes. What Mr. and Mrs. Johnson must have thought of you, I can't imagine, standing there like a stick when they stopped to be civil for a few minutes, and behaving as though you never even heard their asking us to go in and have a bite of supper. What have we done, eh, little Alf and me? You look at us as though we had turned into ogres. Out with it, my man. What's wrong?"

"I am not—"

Burton stopped short. The lie of ill-health stuck in his throat. He thirsted to tell the truth, but a new and gentle kindliness kept him speechless. Ellen was beginning to get a little frightened.

"What is it that's come to you, Alfred?" she again demanded. "Have you lost your tongue or your wits or what?"

"I do not know," he answered truthfully enough. His manner was so entirely non-provocative that her resentment for a moment dropped.

"What's changed you since yesterday?" she persisted. "What is it that you don't like about us, anyway? What do you want us to do?"

Burton sighed. He would have given a great deal to have been able to prevaricate, but he could not. It was the truth alone which he could speak.

"I should like you," he said, "to take down your hair and throw away all that is not real, to wash it until it is its natural color, to brush it hard, and then do it up quite simply, without a net or anything. Then I should like you to wash your face thoroughly in plain soap and water and never again touch a powder-puff or that nasty red stuff you have on your lips. I should like you to throw away those fancy blouses with the imitation lace, which are ugly to start with, and which you can't afford to have washed often enough, and I should like you to buy some plain linen shirts and collars, a black tie, and a blue serge skirt made so that you could walk in it naturally."

Ellen did not at that moment need any rouge, nor any artificial means of lending brightness to her eyes. What she really seemed to need was something to keep her still.

"Anything else?" she demanded, unsteadily.

"Some thicker stockings, or, if not thicker, stockings without that open-work stuff about them," Burton continued earnestly, warming now to his task. "You see, the open-work places have all spread into little holes, and one can't help noticing it, especially as your shoes are such a bright yellow. That stuff that looks like lace at the bottom of your petticoat has got all draggled. I should cut it off and throw it away. Then I'd empty all that scent down the drain, and wear any sort of gloves except those kid ones you have had cleaned so often."

"And my hat?" she asked with trembling lips. "What about my hat? Don't leave that out."

"Burn it," he replied eagerly, "feathers and all. They've been dyed, haven't they? more than once, and I think their present color is their worst. It must be very uncomfortable to wear, too, with all those pins sticking out of it. Colored glass they are made of, aren't they? They are not pretty, you know. I'll buy you a hat, if you like, a plain felt or straw, with just a few flowers. You'll look as nice again."

"Finished?"

He looked at her apprehensively.

"There are one or two things about the house—" he commenced.

Ellen began to talk—simply because she was unable to keep silent any longer. The longer she talked, the more eloquent she became. When she had finished, Burton had disappeared. She followed him to the door, and again to the gate. Her voice was still ringing in his ears as he turned the corner of the street.

IV

A Shock to Mr. Waddington

Punctually at nine o'clock on the following morning, Alfred Burton, after a night spent in a very unsatisfactory lodging-house, hung up his gray Homburg on the peg consecrated to the support of his discarded silk hat, and prepared to plunge into his work. The office-boy, who had been stricken dumb at his senior's appearance, recovered himself at last sufficiently for speech.

"My eye!" he exclaimed. "Whose clothes have you been stealing? What have you been up to, eh? Committing a burglary or a murder?"

Burton shook his head.

"Nothing of the sort," he replied pleasantly. "The fact is I came to the conclusion that my late style of dress, as you yourself somewhat eloquently pointed out yesterday, was unbecoming."

The boy seemed a little dazed.

"You look half way between a toff and an artist!" he declared. "What's it all about, anyway? Have you gone crazy?"

"I don't think so," Burton replied. "I rather think I have come to my senses. Have you got those last furniture accounts?"

"No use starting on that job," Clarkson informed him, genially. "The guvnor wants you down at the salesrooms, you've got to clerk for him."

Burton looked very blank indeed. A flood of unpleasant recollections assailed him. He had lied a good deal in the letting of houses, but he had lied more still in the auction room. And to-day's sale! He knew all about it! He knew a great deal more than under the circumstances it was wise for him to know!

"I quite forgot," he said slowly, "that there was a sale to-day. I don't suppose Mr. Waddington would let you take my place, Clarkson?"

"Not on your life!" the boy replied. "I've got to stay here and boss the show. You'd better hurry along, too. It's Thursday morning and you know the people come in early. Lord, what a guy you look!"

Very slowly and very reluctantly Burton made his way through the gloomy warehouse and into the salesrooms, which were approached from the street by a separate entrance. He knew exactly what was before him and he realized that it must be the end. Mr. Waddington, who had not yet mounted the rostrum, saw him come in, stared at him for several moments in his gray clothes and Homburg hat, and turned away to spit upon the floor. A woman with a catalogue in her hand—evidently an intending purchaser—gripped Burton by the arm.

"I say, mister, you're the auctioneer's clerk, aren't you?"

"I am," he admitted.

"About that h'oil painting, now—the one of Gladstone. My old man's fair dotty on Gladstone and it's his birthday to-morrow. If it's all right, I thought I might make him a present. It says in the catalogue 'Artist unknown.' I suppose, as it's a real oil painting, it's worth a bit, isn't it?"

"It is not an oil painting at all," Burton said quietly.

"Wot yer mean?" the woman demanded. "Here you are—lot number 17—'Interesting oil painting of the Right Honorable W. E. Gladstone, artist unknown.'"

Burton thrust the catalogue away from him with a sigh.

"I am afraid," he admitted, "that the description can scarcely be said to be entirely accurate. As a matter of fact, it is a colored lithograph, very cleverly done but quite valueless. I dare say you would find that there are thousands of them exactly like it."

The woman stared at him suspiciously.

"Why, your guvnor's just told me that the reserve upon it's two guineas!" she exclaimed.

"Mr. Waddington must have made a mistake," Burton replied, with a sinking heart.

"Look here," the woman insisted, "what is it worth, anyway?"

"A few pence for the frame," Burton answered, hurrying off.

The woman drew her shawl about her shoulders, threw her catalogue upon the floor and made her way towards the door.

"Not going to stay here to be swindled!" she declared loudly, looking around her. "Colored lithograph, indeed, and put down in the catalogue as an interesting oil painting! They must think us folks don't know nothing. Cheating's the word, I say—cheating!"

The woman's eye met the eye of Mr. Waddington as she stood for a moment in the doorway before taking her departure. She raised her fist and shook it.

"Bah!" she exclaimed. "Ought to be ashamed of yourself! You and your h'oil paintings!"

Mr. Waddington was too far off to hear her words but the character of her farewell was unmistakable! He glanced suspiciously towards his chief clerk. Burton, however, had at that moment been button-holed by a fidgety old gentleman who desired to ask him a few questions.

"I am a little puzzled, sir," the old gentleman said, confidentially, "about the absolute authenticity of this chippendale suite—lot number 101 in the catalogue. This sale is—er—um—advertised as being—" the old gentleman turned over the pages of the catalogue quickly—"a sale of the effects of the late Doctor Transome. That's so, eh?"

"I believe the announcement is to that effect," Burton confessed, hesitatingly.

"Quite so," the little old gentleman continued. "Now I knew Dr. Transome intimately, and he was, without the slightest doubt, a rare judge of old furniture. I wouldn't mind following him anywhere, or accepting his judgment about anything. He was very set upon not having anything in his house that was not genuine. Now under any other circumstances, mind you, I should have had my doubts about that suite, but if you can assure me that it came from Dr. Transome's house, why, there's no more to be said about it. I'm a bidder."

Burton shook his head gravely.

"I am sorry," he declared, "but the frontispiece of the catalogue is certainly a little misleading. To tell you the truth, sir, there are very few articles here from Dr. Transome's house at all. The bulk of his effects were distributed among relatives. What we have here is a portion of the kitchen and servant's bedroom furniture."

"Then where on earth did all this dining-room and library furniture come from?" the old gentleman demanded.

Burton looked around him and back again at his questioner. There was no evading the matter, however.

"The great majority of it," Burton admitted, "has been sent in to us for sale from dealers and manufacturers."

The little old gentleman was annoyed. Instead of being grateful, as he ought to have been, he visited his annoyance upon Burton, which was unreasonable.

"Deliberate swindling, sir—that's what I call it," he proclaimed, rolling up the catalogue and striking the palm of his hand with it. "All the way from Camberwell I've come, entirely on the strength of what turns out to be a misrepresentation. There's the bus fare there and back—six-pence, mind you—and a wasted morning. Who's going to recompense me, I should like to know? I'm not made of sixpences."

Burton's hand slipped into his pocket. The little old gentleman sniffed.

"You needn't insult me, young fellow," he declared. "I've a friend or two here and I'll set about letting them know the truth."

He was as good as his word. The woman who had departed had also found her sympathizers. Mr. Waddington watched the departure of a little stream of people with a puzzled frown.

"What's the matter with them all?" he muttered. "Come here, Burton."

Burton, who had been standing a little in the background, endeavoring to escape further observation until the commencement of the sale, obeyed his master's summons promptly.

"Can't reckon things up at all," Mr. Waddington confided. "Why aren't you round and amongst 'em, Burton, eh? You're generally such a good 'un at rubbing it into them. Why, the only two people I've seen you talk to this morning have left the place! What's wrong with you, man?"

"I only wish I knew," Burton replied, fervently.

Mr. Waddingon scratched his chin.

"What's the meaning of those clothes, eh?" he demanded. "You've lost your appearance, Burton—that's what you've done. Not even a silk hat on a sale day!"

"I'm sorry," Burton answered. "To tell you the truth, I had forgotten that it was a sale day."

Mr. Waddington looked curiously at his assistant, and the longer he looked, the more convinced he became that Burton was not himself.

"Well," he said, "I suppose you can't always be gassing if you're not feeling on the spot. Let's start the sale before any more people leave. Come on."

Mr. Waddington led the way to the rostrum. Burton, with a sinking heart, and a premonition of evil, took the place by his side. The first few lots were put up and sold without event, but trouble came with lot number 13.

"Lot number 13—a magnificent oak bedroom—" the auctioneer began. "Eh? What? What is it, Burton?"

"Stained deal," Burton interrupted, in a pained but audible whisper. "Stained deal bedroom suite, sir—not oak."

Mr. Waddington seemed about to choke. He ignored the interruption, however, and went on with his description of the lot.

"A magnificent oak bedroom suite, complete and as good as new, been in use for three weeks only. The deceased gentleman whose effects we are disposing of, and who is known to have been a famous collector of valuable furniture, told me himself that he found it at a farmhouse in Northumberland. Look at it, ladies and gentlemen. Look at it. It'll bear inspection. Shall we say forty-five guineas for a start?"

Mr. Waddington paused expectantly. Burton leaned over from his place.

"The suite is of stained deal," he said distinctly. "It has been very cleverly treated by a new process to make it resemble old oak, but if you examine it closely you will see that what I say is correct. I regret that there has been an unfortunate error in the description."

For a moment there was a tumult of voices and some laughter. Mr. Waddington was red in the face. The veins about his temples were swollen and the hammer in his hand showed a desire to descend on his clerk's head. A small dealer had pulled out one of the drawers and was examining it closely.

"Stained deal it is, Mr. Auctioneer," he announced, standing up. "Call a spade a spade and have done with it!"

There was a little mingled laughter and cheers. Mr. Waddington swallowed his anger and went on with the sale.

"Call it what you like," he declared, indulgently. "Our clients send us in these things with their own description and we haven't time to verify them all—not likely. One bedroom suite, then—there you are. Now then, Burton, you blithering idiot," he muttered savagely under his breath, "if you can't hold your tongue I'll kick you out of your seat Thirty pounds shall we say?" he continued, leaning forward persuasively. "Twenty pounds, then? The price makes no difference to me, only do let's get on."

The suite in question was knocked down at eight pounds ten. The sale proceeded, but bidders were few. A spirit of distrust seemed to be in the air. Most of the lots were knocked down to dummy bidders, which meant that they were returned to the manufacturers on the following day. The frown on Mr. Waddington's face deepened.

"See what you've done, you silly jackass!" he whispered to his assistant, during a momentary pause in the proceedings. "There's another little knot of people left. Here's old Sherwell coming in, half drunk. Now hold your tongue if you can. I'll have him for the dining-room suite, sure. If you interfere this time, I'll break your head. . . We come now, ladies and gentlemen, to the most important lot of the day. Mr. Sherwell, sir, I am glad to see you. You're just in time. There's a dining-room suite coming on, the only one I have to offer, and such a suite as is very seldom on the market. One table, two sideboards, and twelve chairs. Now, Mr. Sherwell, sir, look at the table for yourself. You're a judge and I am willing to take your word. Did you ever see a finer, a more magnificent piece of mahogany? There is no deception about it. Feel it, look at it, test it in any way you like. I tell you, ladies and gentlemen, this is a lot I have examined myself, and if I could afford it I'd have bought it privately. I made a bid but the executors wouldn't listen to me. Now then, ladies and gentlemen, make me an offer for the suite."

"Fine bit o' wood," the half-intoxicated furniture dealer pronounced, leaning up against the table and examining it with clumsy gravity. "A genuine bit o' stuff."

"You're right, Mr. Sherwell," the auctioneer agreed, impressively. "It is a unique piece of wood, sir—a unique piece of wood, ladies and gentlemen. Now how much shall we say for the suite? Lot number 85— twelve chairs, the table you are leaning up against, two sideboards, and butler's tray. Shall we say ninety guineas, Mr. Sherwell? Will you start the bidding in a reasonable manner and make it a hundred?"

"Fifty!" Mr. Sherwell declared, striking the table with his fist. "I say fifty!"

Mr. Waddington for a moment looked pained. He laid down the hammer and glanced around through the audience, as though appealing for their sympathy. Then he shrugged his shoulders. Finally, he took up his hammer again and sighed.

"Very well, then," he consented, in a resigned tone, "we'll start it at fifty, then. I don't know what's the matter with every one to-day, but I'm giving you a turn, Mr. Sherwell, and I shall knock it down quick. Fifty guineas is bid for lot number 85. Going at fifty guineas!"

Burton rose once more to his feet.

"Does Mr. Sherwell understand," he asked, "that the remainder of the suite is different entirely from the table?"

Mr. Sherwell stared at the speaker, shifted his feet a little unsteadily and gripped the table.

"Certainly I don't," he replied,—"don't understand anything of the sort! Where is the rest of the suite, young man?"

"Just behind you, sir," Burton pointed out, "up against the wall."

Mr. Sherwell turned and looked at a miserable collection of gimcrack articles piled up against the wall behind him. Then he consulted the catalogue.

"One mahogany dining-table, two sideboards, one butler's tray, twelve chairs. These the chairs?" he asked, lifting one up.

"Those are the chairs, sir," Burton admitted. Mr. Sherwell, with a gesture of contempt, replaced upon the floor the one which he had detached from its fellows. He leaned unsteadily across the table.

"A dirty trick, Mr. Auctioneer," he declared. "Shan't come here any more! Shan't buy anything! Ought to be ashamed of yourself. Yah!"

Mr. Sherwell, feeling his way carefully out, made an impressive if not very dignified exit. Mr. Waddington gripped his clerk by the arm.

"Burton," he hissed under his breath, "get out of this before I throw you down! Never let me see your idiot face again! If you're at the office when I come back, I'll kill you! I'll clerk myself. Be off with you!"

Burton rose quietly and departed. As he left the room, he heard Mr. Waddington volubly explaining that no deception was intended and that the catalogue spoke for itself. Then he passed out into the street and drew a little breath of relief. The shackles had fallen away. He was a free man. Messrs. Waddington & Forbes had finished with him.

V

Burton's New Life

Burton spent the rest of the day in most delightful fashion. He took the Tube to South Kensington Museum, where he devoted himself for several hours to the ecstatic appreciation of a small section of its treasures. He lunched off some fruit and tea and bread and butter out in the gardens, wandering about afterwards among the flower-beds and paying especial and delighted attention to the lilac trees beyond the Memorial. Towards evening he grew depressed. The memory of Ellen, of little Alfred, and his gingerbread villa, became almost like a nightmare to him. And then the light came! His great resolution was formed. With beating heart he turned to a stationer's shop, bought a sheet of paper and an envelope, borrowed a pen and wrote:

> My Dear Ellen,
>
> I am not coming home for a short time. As you remarked, there is something the matter with me. I don't know what it is. Perhaps in a few days I shall find out. I shall send your money as usual on Saturday, and hope that you and the boy will continue well.
>
> From your husband,
> Alfred Burton

Burton sighed a long sigh of intense relief as he folded up and addressed this epistle. Then he bought four stamps and sent it home. He was a free man. He had three pounds fifteen in his pocket, a trifle of money in the savings-bank, no situation, and a wife and son to support. The position was serious enough, yet never for a moment could he regard it without a new elasticity of spirit and a certain reckless optimism, the source of which he did not in the least understand. He was to learn before long, however, that moods and their resulting effect upon the spirit were part of the penalty which he must pay for the greater variety of his new life.

He took a tiny bedroom somewhere Westminster way—a room in a large, solemn-looking house, decayed and shabby, but still showing traces of its former splendor. That night he saw an Ibsen play from the front row of a deserted gallery, and afterwards, in melancholy mood, he walked homeward along the Embankment by the moonlight. For the first time in life he had come face to face with a condition of which he had had no previous experience—the condition of intellectual pessimism. He was depressed because in this new and more spontaneous world, so full of undreamed-of beauties, so exquisitely stimulating to his new powers of appreciation, he had found something which he did not understand. Truth for the first time had seemed unpleasant, not only in its effects but in itself. The problem was beyond him. Nevertheless, he pulled his bed up to the window, from which he could catch a glimpse of the varied lights of the city, and fell asleep.

In the morning he decided to seek for a situation. A very reasonable instinct led him to avoid all such houses as Messrs. Waddington & Forbes. He made his way instead to the offices of a firm who were quite at the top of their profession. A junior partner accorded him a moment's interview. He was civil but to the point.

"There is no opening whatever in this firm," he declared, "for any one who has been in the employment of Messrs. Waddington & Forbes. Good morning!"

On the doorstep, Burton ran into the arms of Mr. Lynn, who recognized him at once.

"Say, young man," he exclaimed, holding out his hand, "I am much obliged for that recommendation of yours to these people! I have taken a house in Connaught Place—a real nice house it is, too. Come and see us—number 17. The wife and daughters land to-morrow."

"Thank you very much," Burton answered. "I am glad you are fixed up comfortably."

Mr. Lynn laid his hand upon the young man's shoulder. He looked at him curiously. He was an observant person and much interested in his fellow-creatures.

"Kind of change in you, isn't there?" he asked, in a puzzled manner. "I scarcely recognized you at first."

Burton made no reply. The conventional falsehood which rose to his lips, died away before it was uttered.

"Look here," Mr. Lynn continued, "you take a word of advice from me. You chuck those people, Waddington & Forbes. They're wrong 'uns—won't do you a bit of good. Get another job. So long, and don't forget to look us up."

Mr. Lynn passed on his way into the office. He ran into the junior partner, who greeted him warmly.

"Say, do you know that young man who's just gone out?" the former inquired.

The junior partner shook his head.

"Never seen him before," he replied. "He came here looking for a job."

"Is that so?" Mr. Lynn asked with interest. "Well, I hope you gave it to him?"

Young Mr. Miller shook his head.

"He came from the wrong school for us," he declared. "Regular thieves, the people he was with. By the bye, didn't they nearly let you that death-trap of old Lady Idlemay's?"

"Yes, and he happens to be just the young man," Mr. Lynn asserted, removing the cigar from his mouth, "who prevented my taking it, or at any rate having to part with a handsome deposit. I was sent down there with him and at first he cracked it up like a real hustler. He got me so fixed that I had practically made up my mind and was ready to sign any reasonable agreement. Then he suddenly seemed to turn round. He looked me straight in the face and told me about the typhoid and all of it, explained that it wasn't the business of the firm to let houses likely to interest me, and wound up by giving me your name and address and recommending me to come to you."

"You surprise me very much indeed," Mr. Miller admitted. "Under the circumstances, it is scarcely to be wondered at that he is out of employment. Old Waddington wouldn't have much use for a man like that."

"I shouldn't be surprised," Mr. Lynn remarked thoughtfully, "if it was through my affair that he got the sack. Couldn't you do something for him, Mr. Miller—to oblige me, eh?"

"If he calls again," Mr. Miller promised, "I will do my best."

But Burton did not call again. He made various efforts to obtain a situation in other directions, without the slightest result. Then he gave it up. He became a wanderer about London, one of her children who watched her with thoughtful eyes at all times and hours of the day and night. He saw the pink dawn glimmer through the trees in St. James's Park. He saw the bridges empty, the smoke-stained buildings deserted by their inhabitants, with St. Paul's in the background like a sentinel watching over the sleeping world. He heard the crash and roar of life die away and he watched like an anxious prophet while the city slept. He looked upon the stereotyped horrors of the Embankment, vitalized and actual to him now in the light of his new understanding. He wandered with the first gleam of light among the flower-beds of the Park, sniffing with joy at the late hyacinths, revelling in the cool, sweet softness of the unpolluted air. Then he listened to the awakening, to the birth of the day. He heard it from the bridges, from London Bridge and Westminster Bridge, over which thundered the great vans fresh from the country, on their way to Covent Garden. He stood in front of the Mansion House and watched the thin, black stream of the earliest corners grow into a surging, black-coated torrent. There were things which made him sorry and there were things which made him glad. On the whole, however, his isolated contemplation of what for so long he had taken as a matter of course depressed him. Life was unutterably and intensely selfish. Every little unit in that seething mass was so entirely, so strangely self-centered. None of them had any real love or friendliness for the millions who toiled around them, no one seemed to have time to take his eyes from his own work and his own interests. Burton became more and more depressed as the days passed. Then he closed his eyes and tried an antidote. He abandoned this study of his fellow-creatures and plunged once more into the museums, sated himself with the eternal beauties, and came out to resume his place amid the tumultuous throng with rested nerves and a beatific smile upon his lips. It mattered so little, his welfare of to-day or to-morrow— whether he went hungry or satisfied to bed! The other things were in his heart. He saw the truth.

One day he met his late employer. Mr. Waddington was not, in his way, an ill-natured man, and he stopped short upon the pavement. Burton's new suit was not wearing well. It showed signs of exposure to the weather. The young man himself was thin and pale. It was not for Mr. Waddington to appreciate the soft brilliance of his eyes, the altered curves of his lips. From his intensely practical point of view, his late employee was certainly in low water.

"Hullo, Burton!" he exclaimed, coming to a standstill and taking the pipe from his mouth.

"How do you do, sir?" Burton replied, civilly.

Getting on all right, eh?

"Very nicely indeed, thank you, sir."

Mr. Waddington grunted.

"Hm! You don't look like it! Got a job yet?"

"No, sir."

"Then how the devil can you be getting on at all?" Mr. Waddington inquired.

Burton smiled quite pleasantly.

"It does seem queer, sir," he admitted. "I said that I was getting on all right because I am contented and happy. That is the chief thing after all, isn't it?"

Mr. Waddington opened his mouth and closed it again.

"I wish I could make out what the devil it was that happened to you," he said. "Why, you used to be as smart as they make 'em, a regular nipper after business. I expected you'd be after me for a partnership before long, and I expect I'd have had to give it you. And then you went clean dotty. I shall never forget that day at the sale, when you began telling people everything it wasn't good for them to know."

"You mean that it wasn't good for us for them to know," Burton corrected gently.

Mr. Waddington laughed. He had a large amount of easy good-humor and he was always ready to laugh.

"You haven't lost your wits, I see," he declared. "What was it? Did you by any chance get religion, Burton?"

The young man shook his head.

"Not particularly, sir," he replied. "By the bye, you owe me four days' money. Would it be quite convenient—?"

"You shall have it," Mr. Waddington declared, thrusting his hand into his trousers pocket. "I can't afford it, for things are going badly with me. Here it is, though. Thirty-four shillings—that's near enough. Anything else?"

"There is one other thing," Burton said slowly. "It is rather a coincidence, sir, that we should have met just here. I see that you have been into Idlemay House. I wonder whether you would lend me the keys? I will return them to the office, with pleasure, but I should very much like to go in myself for a few minutes."

Mr. Waddington stared at his late employee, thoroughly puzzled.

"If you aren't a caution!" he exclaimed. "What the mischief do you want to go in there for?"

Burton smiled.

"I should like to see if that little room where the old Egyptian died has been disturbed since I was there, sir."

Mr. Waddington hesitated. Then he turned and led the way.

"I'd forgotten all about that," he said. "Come along, I'll go in with you."

They crossed the road, ascended the steps, and in a few minutes they were inside the house. The place smelt very musty and uninhabited. Burton delicately avoided the subject of its being still unlet. The little chamber on the right of the hall was as dark as ever. Burton felt his heart beat quickly as a little waft of familiar perfume swept out to him at the opening of the door. Mr. Waddington struck a match and held it over his head.

"So this is the room," he remarked. "Dashed if I've ever been in it! It wants cleaning out and fumigating badly. What's this?"

He picked up the sheet of paper, which was lying exactly as Burton had left it. Then he lifted up the little dwarf tree and looked at it.

"It is finished. The nineteenth generation has triumphed. He who shall eat of the brown fruit of this tree, shall see the things of Life and Death as they are. He who shall eat—"

"Well, I'm d—d!" he muttered. "What's it all mean, anyway?"

"Try a brown bean," Burton suggested softly. "They aren't half bad."

"Very likely poison," Mr. Waddington said, suspiciously.

Burton said nothing for a moment. He had taken up the sheet of paper and was gazing at the untranslated portion.

"I wonder," he murmured, "if there is any one who could tell us what the other part of it means?"

"The d—d thing smells all right," Mr. Waddington declared. "Here goes!"

He broke off a brown bean and swallowed it. Burton turned round just in time to see the deed. For a moment he stood aghast. Then very slowly he tiptoed his way from the door and hurried stealthily from the house. From some bills which he had been studying half an hour ago he remembered that Mr. Waddington was due, later in the morning, to conduct a sale of "antique" furniture!

VI

A Meeting with Ellen

The clearness of vision which enabled Alfred Burton now to live in and appreciate a new and marvelous world, failed, however, to keep him from feeling, occasionally, exceedingly hungry. He lived on very little, but the weekly amount must always be sent to Garden Green. There came a time when he broke in upon the last five pound note of his savings. He realized the position without any actual misgivings. He denied himself regretfully a tiny mezzotint of the Raphael "Madonna," which he coveted for his mantelpiece. He also denied himself dinner for several evenings. When fortune knocked at his door he was, in fact, extraordinarily hungry. He still had faith, notwithstanding his difficulties, and no symptoms of dejection. He was perfectly well aware that this need for food was, after all, one of the most unimportant affairs in the world, although he was forced sometimes to admit to himself that he found it none the less surprisingly unpleasant. Chance, however, handed over to him a shilling discovered upon the curb, and a high-class evening paper left upon a seat in the Park. He had no sooner eaten and drunk with the former than he opened the latter. There was an article on the front page entitled "London Awake." He read it line by line and laughed. It was all so ridiculously simple. He hurried back to his rooms and wrote a much better one on "London Asleep." He was master of his subject. He wrote of what he had seen with effortless and sublime verity. Why not? Simply with the aid of pen and ink he transferred from the cells of his memory into actual phrases the silent panorama which he had seen with his own eyes. That one matchless hour before the dawn was entirely his. Throughout its sixty minutes he had watched and waited with every sense quivering. He had watched and heard that first breath of dawn come stealing into life. It was child's play to him. He knew nothing about editors, but he walked into the office of the newspaper which he had picked up, and explained his mission.

"We are not looking for new contributors at present," he was told a little curtly. "What paper have you been on?"

"I have never written anything before in my life," Burton confessed, "but this is much better than 'London Awake,' which you published a few evenings ago."

The sub-editor of that newspaper looked at him with kindly contempt.

"'London Awake' was written for us by Rupert Mendosa. We don't get beginner's stuff like that. I don't think it will be the least use, but I'll look at your article if you like—quick!"

Burton handed over his copy with calm confidence. It was shockingly written on odd pieces of paper, pinned together anyhow—an untidy and extraordinary-looking production. The sub-editor very nearly threw it contemptuously back. Instead he glanced at it, frowned, read a little more, and went on reading. When he had finished, he looked at this strange, thin young man with the pallid cheeks and deep-set eyes, in something like awe.

"You wrote this yourself?" he asked.

"Certainly, sir," Burton answered. "If it is really worth putting in your paper and paying for, you can have plenty more."

"But why did you write it?" the editor persisted. "Where did you get the idea from?"

Burton looked at him in mild-eyed wonder.

"It is just what I see as I pass along," he explained.

The sub-editor was an ambitious literary man himself and he looked steadfastly away from his visitor, out of the window, his eyes full of regret, his teeth clenched almost in anger. Just what he saw as he passed along! What he saw—this common-looking, half-educated little person, with only the burning eyes and sensitive mouth to redeem him from utter insignificance! Truly this was a strange finger which opened the eyes of some and kept sealed the eyelids of others! For fifteen years this very cultivated gentleman who sat in the sub-editor's chair and drew his two thousand a year, had driven his pen along the scholarly way, and all that he had written, beside this untidy-looking document, had not in it a single germ of the things that count.

"Well?" Burton asked, with ill-concealed eagerness.

The sub-editor was, after all, a man. He set his teeth and came back to the present.

"My readers will, I am sure, find your little article quite interesting," he said calmly. "We shall be glad to accept it, and anything else you may send us in the same vein. You have an extraordinary gift for description."

Burton drew a long sigh of relief.

"Thank you," he said. "How much shall you pay me for it?"

The sub-editor estimated the length of the production. It was not an easy matter, owing to the odd scraps of paper upon which it was written.

"Will ten guineas be satisfactory?" he inquired.

"Very satisfactory indeed," Burton replied, "and I should like it now, at once, please. I need some money to send to my wife."

The sub-editor rang for the cashier.

"So you are married," he remarked. "You seem quite young."

"I am married," Burton admitted. "I am not living with my wife just now because we see things differently. I have also a little boy. They live down at Garden Green and I send them money every Saturday."

"What do you do? What is your occupation?"

"I just wander about," Burton explained. "I used to be an auctioneer's clerk, but I lost my situation and I couldn't get another."

"What made you think of writing?" the sub-editor asked, leaning a little over towards his new contributor.

"I picked up a copy of your newspaper on a seat in the Park," Burton replied. "I saw that article on 'London Awake.' I thought if that sort of thing was worth printing, it was worth paying for, so I tried to do something like it. It is so easy to write just what you see," he concluded, apologetically.

The sub-editor handed him his ten guineas.

"When will you bring me some more work?"

"Whenever you like," Burton replied promptly. "What about?"

The sub-editor shook his head.

"You had better choose your own subjects."

"Covent Garden at half-past three?" Burton suggested, a little diffidently. "I can't describe it properly. I can only just put down what I see going on there, but it might be interesting."

"Covent Garden will do very well indeed," the sub-editor told him. "You needn't bother about the description. Just do as you say; put down—what you see."

Burton put down just what he saw as he moved about the city, for ten days following, and without a word of criticism the sub-editor paid him ten guineas a time and encouraged him to come again. Burton, however, decided upon a few days' rest. Not that the work was any trouble to him; on the contrary it was all too ridiculously easy. It seemed to him the most amazing thing that a description in plain words of what any one might stand and look at, should be called literature. And yet some times, in his more thoughtful moments, he dimly understood. He remembered that between him and the multitudes of his fellow-creatures there was a difference. Everything he saw, he saw through the clear white light. There were no mists to cloud his vision, there was no halo of idealism hovering around the objects upon which his eyes rested. It was the truth he saw, and nothing beyond it. He compared his own work with work of a similar character written by well-known men, and his understanding became more complete. He found in their work a touch of personality, a shade of self-consciousness about the description of even the most ordinary things. The individuality of the writer and his subject were always blended. In his own work, subject alone counted. He had never learned any of the tricks of writing. His prose consisted of the simple use of simple words. His mind was empty of all inheritance of acquired knowledge. He had no preconceived ideals, towards the realizations of which he should bend the things he saw. He was simply a prophet of absolute truth. If he had found in those days a literary godfather, he would, without doubt, have been presented to the world as a genius.

Then, with money in his pocket, clad once more in decent apparel, he made one more effort to do his duty. He sent for Ellen and little Alfred to come up and see him. He sent them a little extra money, and he wrote as kindly as possible. He wanted to do the right thing; he was even anxious about it. He determined that he would do his very best to bridge over that yawning gulf. The gingerbread villa he absolutely could not face, so he met them at the Leicester Square Tube.

The moment they arrived, his heart sank. They stepped out of the lift and looked around them. Ellen's hat seemed larger than ever, and was ornate with violent-colored flowers. Her face was hidden behind a violet veil, and she wore a white feather boa, fragments of which reposed upon the lift man's shoulder and little Alfred's knickerbockers. Her dress was of black velveteen, fitting a little tightly over her corsets, and showing several imperfectly removed stains and creases. She wore tan shoes, one of which was down at the heel, and primrose-colored gloves. Alfred wore his usual black Sunday suit, a lace collar around his neck about a foot wide, a straw hat on the ribbon of which was printed the name of one of His Majesty's battleships, and a curl plastered upon his forehead very much in the style of Burton himself in earlier days. Directly he saw his father, he put his finger in his mouth and seemed inclined to howl. Ellen raised her veil and pushed him forward.

"Run to daddy," she ordered, sharply. "Do as you're told, or I'll box your ears."

The child made an unwilling approach. Ellen herself advanced, holding her skirts genteelly clutched in her left hand, her eyes fixed upon her husband, her expression a mixture of defiance and appeal. Burton welcomed them both calmly. His tongue failed him, however, when he tried to embark upon the most ordinary form of greeting. Their appearance gave him again a most unpleasant shock, a fact which he found it extremely difficult to conceal.

"Well, can't you say you're glad to see us?" Ellen demanded, belligerently.

"If I had not wished to see you," he replied, tactfully, "I should not have asked you to come."

"Kiss your father," Ellen ordered, twisting the arm of her offspring. "Kiss him at once, then, and stop whimpering."

The salute, which seemed to afford no one any particular satisfaction, was carried out in perfunctory fashion. Burton, secretly wiping his lips—he hated peppermint—turned towards Piccadilly.

"We will have some tea," he suggested,—"Lyons', if you like. There is music there. I am glad that you are both well."

"Considering," Ellen declared, "that you haven't set eyes on us for Lord knows how long—well, you need to be glad. Upon my word!"

She was regarding her husband in a puzzled manner. Burton was quietly but well dressed. His apparel was not such as Ellen would have thought of choosing for him, but in a dim sort of way she recognized its qualities. She recognized, too, something new about him which, although she vigorously rebelled against it, still impressed her with a sense of superiority.

"Alfred Burton," she continued, impressively, "for the dear land's sake, what's come over you? Mrs. Johnson was around last week and told me you'd lost your job at Waddington's months ago. And here you are, all in new clothes, and not a word about coming back or anything. Am I your wife or not? What do you mean by it? Have you gone off your head, or what have we done—me and little Alfred?"

"We will talk at tea-time," Burton said, uneasily.

Ellen set her lips grimly and the little party hastened on. Burton ordered an extravagant tea, in which Ellen declined to take the slightest interest. Alfred alone ate stolidly and with every appearance of complete satisfaction. Burton had chosen a place as near the band as possible, with a view to rendering conversation more or less difficult. Ellen, however, had a voice which was superior to bands. Alfred, with his mouth continually filled with bun, appeared fascinated by the cornet player, from whom he seldom removed his eyes.

"What I want to know, Alfred Burton, is first how long this tomfoolery is to last, and secondly what it all means?" Ellen began, with her elbows upon the table and a reckless disregard of neighbors. "Haven't we lived for ten years, husband and wife, at Clematis Villa, and you as happy and satisfied with his home as a man could be? And now, all of a sudden, comes this piece of business. Have you gone off your head? Here are all the neighbors just wild with curiosity, and I knowing no more what to say to them than the man in the moon."

"Is there any necessity to say anything to them?" Burton asked, a little vaguely.

Ellen shook in her chair. A sham tortoise-shell hairpin dropped from her untidy hair on to the floor with a little clatter. Her veil parted at the top from her hat. Little Alfred, terrified by an angry frown from the cornet player, was hastily returning fragments of partially consumed bun to his plate. The air of the place was hot and uncomfortable. Burton for a moment half closed his eyes. His whole being was in passionate revolt.

"Any necessity?" Ellen repeated, half hysterically. "Alfred Burton, let's have done with this shilly-shallying! After coming home regularly to your meals for six years, do you suppose you can disappear and not have people curious? Do you suppose you can leave your wife and son and not a word said or a question asked? What I want to know is this— are you coming home to Clematis Villa or are you not?"

"At present I am not," Burton declared, gently but very firmly indeed.

"Is it true that you've got the sack from Mr. Waddington?"

"Perfectly," he admitted. "I have found some other work, though."

She leaned forward so that one of those dyed feathers to which he objected so strongly brushed his cheek.

"Have you touched the money in the Savings Bank?" she demanded.

"I have drawn out every penny of it to send you week by week," he replied, "but I am in a position now to replace it. You can do it yourself, in your own name, if you like. Here it is."

He produced a little roll of notes and handed them to her. She took them with shaking fingers. She was beginning to lose some of her courage. The sight of the money impressed her.

"Alfred Burton," she said, "why don't you drop all this foolishness? Come home with us this afternoon."

She leaned across the table, on which she had once more plumped her elbows. She looked at him in a way he had once found fascinating—her chin thrown forward, her cheeks supported by her knuckles. Little specks of her boa fell into her untouched teacup.

"Come home with Alfred and me," she begged, with half-ashamed earnestness. "It's band night and we might ask the Johnsons in to supper. I've got a nice steak in the house, been hanging, and Mrs. Cross could come in and cook it while we are out. Mr. Johnson would sing to us afterwards, and there's your banjo. You do play it so well, Alfred. You used to like band nights—to look forward to them all the week. Come, now!"

The man's whole being was in a state of revolt. It was an amazing thing indeed, this which had come to him. No wonder Ellen was puzzled! She had right on her side, and more than right. It was perfectly true that he had been accustomed to look forward to band nights. It was true that he used to like to have a neighbor in to supper afterwards, and play the fool with the banjo and crack silly jokes; talk shop with Johnson, who was an auctioneer's clerk himself; smoke atrocious cigars and make worse puns. And now! He looked at her almost pitifully.

"I—I can't manage it just yet," he said, hurriedly. "I'll write—or see you again soon. Ellen, I'm sorry," he wound up, "but just at present I can't change anything."

So Burton paid the bill and the tea-party was over. He saw them off as far as the lift in Leicester Square Station, but Ellen never looked at him again. He had a shrewd suspicion that underneath her veil she was weeping. She refused to say good-bye and kept tight hold of Alfred's hand. When they had gone, he passed out of the station and stood upon the pavement of Piccadilly Circus. Side by side with a sense of immeasurable relief, an odd kind of pain was gripping his heart. Something that had belonged to him had been wrenched away. A wave of meretricious sentiment, false yet with a curious base of naturalness, swept in upon him for a moment and tugged at his heart-strings. She had been his woman; the little boy with the sticky mouth was child of his. The bald humanity of his affections for them joined forces for a moment with the simple greatness of his new capacity. Dimly he realized that somewhere behind all these things lurked a truth greater than any he had as yet found. Then, with an almost incredible swiftness, this new emotion began to fade away. His brain began to work, his new fastidiousness asserted itself. A wave of cheap perfume assailed his nostrils. The untidy pretentiousness of her ill-chosen clothes, the unreality of her manner and carriage, the sheer vulgarity of her choice of words and phrases—these things seized him as a nightmare. Like a man who rushes to a cafe for a drink in a moment of exhaustion, he hastened along towards the National Gallery. His nerves were all quivering. An opalescent light in the sky above Charing Cross soothed him for a moment. A glimpse into a famous art shop was like a cool draught of water. Then, as he walked along in more leisurely fashion, the great idea came to him. He stopped short upon the pavement. Here was the solution to all his troubles: a bean for Ellen; another, or perhaps half of one, for little Alfred! He could not go back to their world; he would bring them into his!

VII

The Truthful Auctioneer

At a little before ten on the following morning, Burton stood upon the pavement outside, looking with some amazement at the house in Wenslow Square. The notices "To Let" had all been torn down. A small army of paper-hangers and white-washers were at work. A man was busy fastening flower boxes in the lower windows. On all hands were suggestions of impending occupation. Burton mounted the steps doubtfully and stood in the hall, underneath a whitewasher's plank. The door of the familiar little room stood open before him. He peered eagerly in. It was swept bare and completely empty. All traces of its former mysterious occupant were gone.

"Is this house let?" he inquired of a man who was deliberately stirring a pail of shiny whitewash.

The plasterer nodded.

"Seems so," he admitted. "It's been empty long enough."

Burton looked around him a little vaguely.

"You all seem very busy," he remarked.

"Some bloke from the country's taken the 'ouse," the man grumbled, "and wants to move in before the blooming paint's dry. Nobody can't do impossibilities, mister," he continued, "leaving out the Unions, which can't bear to see us over-exert ourselves. They've always got a particular eye on me, knowing I'm a bit too rapid for most of them when I start."

"Give yourself a rest for a moment," Burton begged. "Tell me, what's become of the rugs and oddments of furniture from that little room opposite?"

The man produced a pipe, contemplated it for a moment thoughtfully, and squeezed down a portion of blackened tobacco with his thumb.

"Poor smoking," he complained. "Got such a family I can't afford more than one ounce a week. Nothing but dust here."

"I haven't any tobacco with me," Burton regretted, "but I'll stand a couple of ounces, with pleasure," he added, producing a shilling.

The man pocketed the coin without undue exhilaration, struck a vilely smelling match, and lit the fragment of filth at the bottom of his pipe.

"About those oddments of furniture?" Burton reminded him.

"Stolen," the man asserted gloomily,—"stolen under our very eyes, as it were. Some one must have nipped in just as you did this morning, and whisked them off. Easy done with a covered truck outside and us so wrapped up in our work, so to speak."

"When was this?" Burton demanded, eagerly.

"Day afore yesterday."

"Does Mr. Waddington know about it?"

The man removed his pipe from his teeth and gazed intently at his questioner.

"Is this Mr. Waddington you're a-speaking of a red-faced gentleman—kind of auctioneer or agent? Looks as though he could shift a drop?"

Burton recognized the description.

"That," he assented, "is Mr. Waddington."

The workman replaced the pipe in the corner of his mouth and nodded deliberately.

"He knows right enough, he does. Came down here yesterday afternoon with a friend. Seemed, from what I could hear, to want to give him something to eat out of that room. I put him down as dotty, but my! you should have heard him when he found out that the stuff had been lifted!"

"Was he disappointed?" Burton asked.

Words seemed to fail the plasterer. He nodded his head a great many times and spat upon the floor.

"That may be the word I was looking for," he admitted. "Can't say as I should have thought of it myself. Anyway, the bloke never stopped for close on five minutes, and old Joe—him on the ladder there—he came all the way down and listened with his mouth open, and he don't want no laming neither when there's things to be said. Kind of auctioneer they said he was. Comes easy to that sort, I suppose."

"Did he—did Mr. Waddington obtain any clue as to the whereabouts of the missing property?" Burton asked, with some eagerness.

"Not as I knows on," the plasterer replied, picking up his brush, "and as to the missing property, there was nowt but a few mouldy rugs and a flower-pot in the room. Some folks does seem able to work themselves up into a fuss about nothing, and no mistake! Good morning, guvnor! Drop in again some time when you're passing."

Burton turned out of Wenslow Square and approached the offices and salesrooms of Messrs. Waddington & Forbes with some misgiving.

Bearing in mind the peculiar nature of the business conducted by the firm, he could only conclude that ruin, prompt and absolute, had been the inevitable sequence of Mr. Waddington's regrettable appetite. He was somewhat relieved to find that there were no evidences of it in the familiar office which he entered with some diffidence.

"Is Mr. Waddington in?" he inquired.

A strange young man slipped from his stool and found his questioner gazing about him in a bewildered manner. There was much, indeed, that was surprising in his surroundings. The tattered bills had been torn down from the walls, the dust-covered files of papers removed, the ceilings and walls painted and papered. A general cleanliness and sense of order had taken the place of the old medley. The young man who had answered his inquiry was quietly dressed and not in the least like the missing office-boy.

"Mr. Waddington is at present conducting a sale of furniture," he replied. "I can send a message in if your business is important."

Burton, who had always felt a certain amount of liking for his late employer, was filled now with a sudden pity for him. Truth was a great and marvelous thing, but the last person who had need of it was surely an auctioneer engaged in the sale of sham articles of every description! It was putting the man in an unfair position. A vague sense of loyalty towards his late chief prompted Burton's next action. If help were possible, Mr. Waddington should have it.

"Thank you," he said, "I will step into the sales-room myself. I know the way."

Burton pushed open the doors and entered the room. To his surprise, the place was packed. There was the usual crowd of buyers and many strange faces; the usual stacks of furniture of the usual quality, and other lots less familiar. Mr. Waddington stood in his accustomed place but not in his accustomed attitude. The change in him was obvious but in a sense pathetic. He was quietly dressed, and his manner denoted a new nervousness, not to say embarrassment. Drops of perspiration stood upon his forehead. The strident note had gone from his voice. He spoke clearly enough, but more softly, and without the familiar roll.

"Gentlemen—ladies and gentlemen," he was saying as Burton entered, "the next item on the catalogue is number 17, described as an oak chest, said to have come from Winchester Cathedral and to be a genuine antique."

Mr. Waddington leaned forward from his rostrum. His tone became more earnest.

"Ladies and gentlemen," he continued, "I am bound to sell as per catalogue, and the chest in question is described exactly as it was sent in to us, but I do not myself for a moment believe either that it came from Winchester or that it is in any way antique. Examine it for yourselves—pray examine it thoroughly before you bid. My impression is that it is a common oak chest, treated by the modern huckster whose business it is to make new things look like old. I have told you my opinion, ladies and gentlemen. At what shall we start the bidding? It is a useful article, anyhow, and might pass for an antique if any one here really cares to deceive his friends. At any rate, there is no doubt that it is—er—a chest, and that it will—er—hold things. How much shall we say for it?"

There was a little flutter of conversation. People elbowed one another furiously in their desire to examine the chest. A dark, corpulent man, with curly black hair and an unmistakable nose, looked at the auctioneer in a puzzled manner.

"Thay, Waddington, old man, what'th the game, eh? What have you got up your sleeve that you don't want to thell the stuff? Blow me if I can tumble to it!"

"There is no game at all," Mr. Waddington replied firmly. "I can assure you, Mr. Absolom, and all of you, ladies and gentlemen, that I have simply told you what I believe to be the absolute truth. It is my business to sell whatever is sent to me here for that purpose, but it is not my business or intention to deceive you in any way, if I can help it."

Mr. Absolom re-examined the oak chest with a puzzled expression. Then he strolled away and joined a little knot of brokers who were busy discussing matters. The various remarks which passed from one to another indicated sufficiently their perplexed condition of mind.

"The old man's dotty!"

"Not he! There's a game on somewhere!"

"He wants to buy in some of the truck!"

"Old Waddy knows what he's doing!"

Mr. Absolom listened for a while and then returned to the rostrum.

"Mr. Waddington," he asked, "ith it the truth that there are one or two pieces of real good stuff here, thent in by an old farmer in Kent?"

"Quite true," Mr. Waddington declared, eagerly. "Unfortunately, they all came in together and were included with other articles which have not the same antecedents. You may be able to pick out which they are. I can't. Although I am supposed to be in the business, I never could tell the difference myself."

There was a chorus of guffaws. Mr. Waddington mopped his forehead with a handkerchief.

"It is absolutely true, gentlemen," he pleaded. "I have always posed as a judge but I know very little about it. As a matter of fact I have had scarcely any experience in real antique furniture. We must get on, gentlemen. What shall we say for lot number 17? Will any one start the bidding at one sovereign?"

"Two!" Mr. Absolom offered. "More than it'th worth, perhaps, but I'll rithk it."

"It is certainly more than it's worth," Mr. Waddington admitted, dolefully. "However, if you have the money to throw away—two pounds, then."

Mr. Waddington raised his hammer to knock the chest down, but was met with a storm from all quarters of the room.

"Two-ten!"

"Three!"

"Three-ten!"

"Four!"

"Four-ten!"

"Five!"

"Six pounds!"

"Seven!"

"Seven-ten!"

"Ten pounds!"

Mr. Absolom, who so far had held his own, hesitated at the last bid. A gray-haired old gentleman looked around him fiercely. The gentleman was seemingly opulent and Mr. Absolom withdrew with a sigh. Mr. Waddington eyed the prospective buyer sorrowfully.

"You are quite sure that you mean it, sir?" he asked. "The chest is not worth the money, you know."

"You attend to your business and I'll attend to mine!" the old gentleman answered, savagely. "Most improper behavior, I call it, trying to buy in your own goods in this bare-faced manner. My name is Stephen Hammonde, and the money's in my pocket for this or anything else I care to buy."

Mr. Waddington raised his hammer and struck the desk in front of him. As his clerk entered the sale, the auctioneer looked up and caught Burton's eye. He beckoned to him eagerly. Burton came up to the rostrum.

"Burton," Mr. Waddington exclaimed, "I want to talk to you! You see what's happened to me?" he went on, mopping his forehead with his handkerchief.

"Yes, I see!

"It's that d—d bean!" Mr. Waddington declared. "But look here, Burton, can you tell me what's happened to the other people?"

"I cannot," Burton confessed. "I am beginning to get an idea, perhaps."

"Stand by for a bit and watch," Mr. Waddington begged. "I must go on with the sale now. Take a little lunch with me afterwards. Don't desert me, Burton. We're in this together."

Burton nodded and found a seat at a little distance from the rostrum. From here he watched the remainder of the morning's sale. The whole affair seemed to resolve itself into a repetition of the sale of the chest. The auctioneer's attempts to describe correctly the wares he offered were met with mingled suspicion and disbelief. The one or two articles which really had the appearance of being genuine, and over which he hesitated, fetched enormous prices, and all the time his eager clients eyed him suspiciously. No one trusted him, and yet it was obvious that if he had advertised a sale every day, the room would have been packed. Burton watched the proceedings with the utmost interest. Once or twice people who recognized him came up and asked him questions, to which, however, he was able to return no satisfactory reply. At one o'clock precisely, the auctioneer, with a little sigh of relief, announced a postponement. Even after he had left the rostrum, the people seemed unwilling to leave the place.

"Back again this afternoon, sir?" some one called out.

"At half-past two," the auctioneer replied, with a smothered groan.

VIII

HESITATION

Mr. Waddington called a taxicab.

"I can't stand the Golden Lion any longer," he explained. "Somehow or other, the place seems to have changed in the most extraordinary manner' during the last week or so. Everybody drinks too much there. The table-linen isn't clean, and the barmaids are too familiar. I've found out a little place in Jermyn Street where I go now when I have time. We can talk there."

Burton nodded. He was, as a matter of fact, intensely interested. Only a few weeks ago, his late employer had spent nearly every moment of his time, when his services were not urgently required at the office, at the Golden Lion, and he had been seen on more than one occasion at the theatre and elsewhere with one or another of the golden-haired ladies behind the bar. Mr. Waddington—fortunately, perhaps, considering his present predicament!—was a bachelor.

The restaurant, if small, was an excellent one, and Mr. Waddington, who seemed already to be treated with the consideration of a regular customer, ordered a luncheon which, simple though it was, inspired his companion with respect. The waiter withdrew and the auctioneer and his quondam clerk sat and looked at one another. Their eyes were full of questions. Mr. Waddington made a bad lapse.

"What in hell do you suppose it all means, Burton?" he demanded. "You see, I've got it too!"

"Obviously," Burton answered. "I am sure," he added, a little hesitatingly, "that I congratulate you."

Mr. Waddington at that moment looked scarcely a subject for congratulation. A spasm, as though of pain, had suddenly passed across his face. He clutched at the sides of his chair.

"It's marvelous!" he murmured. "A single word like that and I suffer in an absolutely indescribable sort of way. There seems to be something pulling at me all the time, even when it rises to my lips."

"I shouldn't worry about that," Burton replied. "You must get out of the habit. It's quite easy. I expect very soon you will find all desire to use strong language has disappeared entirely."

Mr. Waddington was inclined to be gloomy.

"That's all very well," he declared, "but I've my living to get."

"You seem to be doing pretty well up to now," Burton reminded him.

Mr. Waddington assented, but without enthusiasm.

"It can't last, Burton," he said. "I am ashamed to say it, but all my crowd have got so accustomed to hear me—er—exaggerate, that they disbelieve everything I say as a matter of habit. I tell them now that the goods I am offering are not what they should be, because I can't help it, and they think it's because I have some deep game up my sleeve, or because I do not want to part. I give them a week or so at the most, Burton—no more."

"Don't you think," Burton suggested doubtfully, "that there might be an opening in the profession for an auctioneer who told the truth?"

Mr. Waddington smiled sadly.

"That's absurd, Burton," he replied, "and you know it."

Burton considered the subject thoughtfully.

"There must be occupations," he murmured, "where instinctive truthfulness would be an advantage."

"I can't think of one," Mr. Waddington answered, gloomily. "Besides, I am too old for anything absolutely new."

"How on earth did you succeed in letting Idlemay House?" Burton asked suddenly.

"Most remarkable incident," his host declared. "Reminds me of my last two sales of antique furniture. This man—a Mr. Forrester—came to me with his wife, very keen to take a house in that precise neighborhood. I asked him the lowest rent to start with, and I told him that the late owner had died of typhoid there, and that the drains had practically not been touched since."

"And yet he took it?"

"Took it within twenty-four hours," Mr. Waddington continued. "He seemed to like the way I put it to him, and instead of being scared he went to an expert in drains, who advised him that there was only quite a small thing wrong. He's doing up some of the rooms and moving in in a fortnight."

"This sounds as though there might be an opening for an honest house-agent," Burton suggested.

Mr. Waddington looked dubious.

"It's never been tried. Just this once it came off, but as a regular thing I should have no confidence in it. People like to be gulled. They've been brought up to it. They ask for lies—that's why the world's so full of them. Case of supply and demand, you know."

"According to you, then," Burton remarked, a little dolefully, "it seems as though this change in us unfits us for any sort of practical life."

Mr. Waddington coughed. Even his cough was no longer strident.

"That," he confessed, "has been worrying me. I find it hard to see the matter differently. If one might venture upon a somewhat personal question, how did you manage to discover a vocation? You seem to be prospering," he added, glancing at his companion's neat clothes and gray silk tie.

"I was fortunate," Burton admitted frankly. "I discovered quite by accident the one form in which it is possible to palm off the truth on an unsuspecting public."

Mr. Waddington laid down his knife and fork. He was intensely interested.

"Art," Burton murmured softly.

"Art?" Mr. Waddington echoed under his breath, a little vaguely. The questioning gleam was still in his eyes.

"Painting, sculpture, in my case writing," Burton explained. "I read something when I was half starving which was in a newspaper and had obviously been paid for, and I saw at once that the only point about it was that the man had put down what he saw instead of what he thought he saw. I tried the same thing, and up to the present, at any rate, it seems to go quite Well."

"That's queer," Mr. Waddington murmured. "Do you know," he continued, dropping his voice and looking around him anxiously, "that I've taken to reading Ruskin? I've got a copy of 'The Seven Lamps' at the office, and I can't keep away from it. I slip it into my drawer if any one comes in, like an office boy reading the Police Gazette. All the time I am in the streets I am looking at the buildings, and, Burton, this is the extraordinary part of it, I know no more about architecture than a babe unborn, and yet I can tell you where they're wrong, every one of them. There are some streets I can't pass through, and I close my eyes whenever I get near Buckingham Palace. On the other hand, I walked a mile the other day to see a perfect arch down in South Kensington, and there are some new maisonettes in Queen Anne Street without a single erring line."

Burton poured himself out a glass of wine from the bottle which his companion had ordered.

"Mr. Waddington," he said, "this is a queer thing that has happened to us."

"Not a soul would believe it," the auctioneer assented. "No one will ever believe it. The person who declared that there was nothing new under the sun evidently knew nothing about these beans!"

Burton leaned across the table.

"Mr. Waddington," he continued, "I was around at Idlemay House this morning. I went to see what had become of the flower-pot. I found the little room swept bare. One of the workmen told me that the things had been stolen."

Mr. Waddington showed some signs of embarrassment. He waited for his companion to proceed.

"I wanted the rest of those beans," Burton confessed.

Mr. Waddington shook his head slowly.

"I haven't made up my mind about them yet," he said. "Better leave them alone."

"You do know where they are, then?" Burton demanded breathlessly.

The auctioneer did not deny it.

"I had them removed," he explained "in a somewhat peculiar fashion. The fact of it is, the new tenant is a very peculiar man and I did not dare to ask him to give me that little tree. I simply did not dare to run the risk. It is a painful subject with me, this, because quite thoughtlessly I endeavored to assume the appearance of anger on discovering the theft. The words nearly stuck in my throat and I was obliged to lie down for an hour afterwards."

BURTON DREW A LITTLE BREATH of relief.

"I wish I'd asked you about this before," he declared. "I should have enjoyed my luncheon better."

Mr. Waddington coughed.

"The beans," he remarked, "are in my possession. There are only eleven of them and I have not yet made up my mind exactly what to do with them."

"Mr. Waddington," Burton said impressively, "have you forgotten that I am a married man?"

Mr. Waddington started.

"God bless my soul!" he exclaimed. "I had forgotten that!"

"A wife and one little boy," Burton continued. "We were living at Garden Green in a small plastered edifice called Clematis Villa.

My wife is a vigorous woman, part of whose life has been spent in domestic service, and part in a suburban dressmaker's establishment. She keeps the house very clean, pins up the oleographs presented to us at Christmas time by the grocer and the oil-man, and thinks I look genteel in a silk hat when we walk out to hear the band in the public gardens on Thursday evenings."

"I can see her!" Mr. Waddington groaned. "My poor fellow!"

"She cuts out her own clothes," Burton continued, "from patterns presented by a ladies' penny paper. She trims her own hats with an inheritance of feathers which, in their day have known every color of the rainbow. She loves strong perfumes, and she is strenuous on the subject of the primary colors. We have a table-cloth with fringed borders for tea on Sunday afternoons. She hates flowers because they mess up the rooms so, but she adorns our parlor with wool-work mementoes, artificial roses under a glass case, and crockery neatly inscribed with the name of some seaside place."

Mr. Waddington wiped the perspiration from his forehead and produced a small silver casket from his waistcoat pocket.

"Stop!" he begged. "You win! I can see what you are aiming at. Here is a bean."

Burton waved it away.

"Listen," he proceeded. "I have also a child—a little son. His name is Alfred. He is called Alf, for short. His mother greases his hair and he has a curl which comes over his forehead. I have never known him when his hands were not both sticky and dirty—his hands and his lips. On holidays he wears a velveteen suit with grease spots inked over, an imitation lace collar, and a blue make-up tie."

Mr. Waddington re-opened the silver casket.

"It is Fate," he decided. "Here are two beans." Burton folded them up in a piece of paper and placed them carefully in his waistcoat pocket.

"I felt convinced," he said gratefully, "that I should not make my appeal to you in vain. Tell me, what do you think of doing with the rest?"

"I am not sure," Mr. Waddington admitted, after a brief pause. "We are confronted from the beginning with the fact that there isn't a living soul who would believe our story. If we tried to publish it, people would only look upon it as an inferior sort of fiction, and declare that the idea had been used before. I thought of having one of the beans resolved into its constituents by a scientific physician, but I doubt if I'd get any one to treat the matter seriously. Of course," he went on, "if there were any quantity of the beans, so that we could prove the truth of our statements upon any one who professed to doubt them, we might be able to put them to some practical use. At present," he concluded, with a little sigh, "I really can't think of any."

"When one considers," Burton remarked, "the number of people in high positions who might have discovered these beans and profited by them, it does rather appear as though they had been wasted upon an auctioneer and an auctioneer's clerk who have to get their livings."

"I entirely agree with you," Mr. Waddington assented. "I must admit that in some respects I feel happier and life seems a much more interesting place. Yet I can't altogether escape from certain apprehensions as regards the future."

"If you take my advice," Burton said firmly, "you'll continue the business exactly as you are doing at present."

"I have no idea of abandoning it," Mr. Waddington replied. "The trouble is, how long will it be before it abandons me?"

"I have a theory of my own as to that," Burton declared. "We will not talk about it at present—simply wait and see."

Mr. Waddington paid the bill.

"Meanwhile," he said, "you had better get down to Garden Green as quickly as you can. You will excuse me if I hurry off? It is almost time to start the sale again."

Burton followed his host into the street. The sun was shining, and a breath of perfume from the roses in a woman's gown assailed him, as she passed by on the threshold to enter the restaurant. He stood quite still for a moment. He had succeeded in his object, he had acquired the beans which were to restore to him his domestic life, and in place of any sense of satisfaction he was conscious of an intense sense of depression. What magic, after all, could change Ellen! He forgot for one moment the gulf across which he had so miraculously passed. He thought of himself as he was now, and of Ellen as she had been. The memory of that visit to Garden Green seemed suddenly like a nightmare. The memory of the train, underground for part of the way, with its stuffy odors, made him shiver. The hot, dusty, unmade street, with its hideous rows of stuccoed villas, loomed before his eyes and confirmed his swiftly born disinclination to taking at once this final and ominous step. Something all the time seemed to be drawing him in another direction, the faint magic of a fragrant memory—a dream, was it—that he had carried with him unconsciously through a wilderness of empty days? He hesitated, and finally climbed up on to the garden seat of an omnibus on its way to Victoria.

IX

The Land of Enchantment

I do not think," the girl with the blue eyes said, diffidently, "that I gave you permission to sit down here."

"I do not believe," Burton admitted, "that I asked for it. Still, having just saved your life—"

"Saved my life!"

"Without a doubt," Burton insisted, firmly. She laughed in his face. When she laughed, she was good to look upon. She had firm white teeth, light brown hair which fell in a sort of fringe about her forehead, and eyes which could be dreamy but were more often humorous. She was not tall and she was inclined to be slight, but her figure was lithe, full of beautiful spring and reach.

"You drove away a cow!" she exclaimed. "It is only because I am rather idiotic about cows that I happened to be afraid. I am sure that it was a perfectly harmless animal."

"On the contrary," he assured her seriously, "there was something in the eye of that cow which almost inspired me with fear. Did you notice the way it lashed its tail?"

"Absurd!"

"At least," he protested, "you cannot find it absurd that I prefer to sit here with you in the shadow of your lilac trees, to trudging any further along that dusty road?"

"You haven't the slightest right to be here at all," she reminded him. "I didn't even invite you to come in."

He sighed.

"Women have so little sense of consequence," he murmured. "When you came in through that gate without saying good-bye, I naturally concluded that I was expected to follow, especially as you had just pointed this out to me as being your favorite seat."

Again she laughed. Then she stopped suddenly and looked at him. He really was a somewhat difficult person to place.

"If I hadn't a very irritable parent to consider," she declared, "I think I should ask you to tea."

Burton looked very sad.

"You need not have put it into my head," he objected gently. "The inn smells so horribly of the beer that other people have drunk. Besides, I have come such a long way—just for a glimpse of you."

It seemed to her like a false note. She frowned.

"That," she insisted, "is ridiculous."

"Is it?" he murmured. "Don't you ever, when you walk in your gardens, with only that low wall between you and the road, wonder whether any of those who pass by may not carry away a little vision with them? It is a beautiful setting, you know."

"The people who pass by are few," she answered. "We are too far off the beaten track. Only on Saturdays and holiday times there are trippers, fearful creatures who pick the bracken, walk arm in arm, and sing songs. Tell me why you look as though you were dreaming, my preserver?"

"Look along the lane," he said softly. "Can't you see them—the wagonette with the tired horse drawn up just on the common there—a tired, dejected-looking horse, with a piece of bracken tied on to his head to keep the flies off? There were three men, two women and a little boy. They drank beer and ate sandwiches behind that gorse bush there. They called one another by their Christian names, they shouted loud personal jokes, one of the women sang. She wore a large hat with dyed feathers. She had black, untidy-looking hair, and her face was red. One of the men made a noise with his lips as an accompaniment. There was the little boy, too—a pasty-faced little boy with a curl on his forehead, who cried because he had eaten too much. One of the men sat some distance apart from the others and stared at you—stared at you for quite a long time."

"I remember it perfectly," she declared. "It was last Whit-Monday. Hateful people they were, all of them. But how did you know? I saw nobody else pass by."

"I was there," he whispered.

"And I never saw you!" she exclaimed in wonder. "I remember those Bank Holiday people, though, how abominable they were."

"You saw me," he insisted gently. "I was the one who sat apart and stared."

"Of course you are talking rubbish!" she asserted, uneasily.

He shook his head.

"I was behind the banks—the banks of cloud, you know," he went on, a little wistfully. "I think that that was one of the few moments in my life when I peered out of my prison-house. I must have known what was coming. I must have remembered afterwards—for I came here."

She looked at him doubtfully. Her eyes were very blue and he looked into them steadfastly. By degrees the lines at the sides of her mouth began to quiver.

"Why, that person was abominable!" she declared. "He stared at me as though I were something unreal. He had taken off his coat and rolled his shirt sleeves up. He had on bright yellow boots and a hateful necktie. You, indeed! I would as soon believe," she concluded, "that you had fallen, to-day from a flying-machine."

"Let us believe that," he begged, earnestly. "Why not? Indeed, in a sense it is true. I am cut adrift from my kind, a stroller through life, a vagabond without any definite place or people. I am trying to teach myself the simplest forms of philosophy. To-day the sky is so blue and the wind blows from the west and the sun is just hot enough to draw the perfume from the gorse and the heather. Come and walk with me over the moors. We will race the shadows, for surely we can move quicker than those fleecy little morsels of clouds!"

"Certainly not," she retorted, with a firmness which was suspiciously emphasized. "I couldn't think of walking anywhere with a person whom I didn't know! And besides, I have to go and make tea in a few minutes."

He looked over her shoulder and sighed. A trim parlor maid was busy arranging a small table under the cedar tree.

"Tea!" he murmured. "It is unfortunate."

"Not at all!" she replied sharply. "If you'd behave like a reasonable person for five minutes, I might ask you to stay."

"A little instruction?" he pleaded. "I am really quite apt. My apparent stupidity is only misleading."

"You may be, as you say, a vagabond and an outcast, and all that sort of thing, but this is a conventional English home," the girl with the blue eyes declared, "and I am a perfectly well-behaved young woman with an absent-minded but strict parent. I could not think of asking any one to tea of whose very name I was ignorant."

He pointed to the afternoon paper which lay at her feet.

"I sign myself there 'A Passer-by.' My real name is Burton. Until lately I was an auctioneer's clerk. Now I am a drifter—what you will."

"You wrote those impressions of St. James's Park at dawn?" she asked eagerly.

"I did."

She smiled a smile of relief.

"Of course I knew that you were a reasonable person," she pronounced. "Why couldn't you have said so at once? Come along to tea."

"Willingly," he replied, rising to his feet. "Is this your father coming across the lawn?"

She nodded.

"He's rather a dear. Do you know anything about Assyria?"

"Not a scrap."

"That's a pity," she regretted. "Come. Father, this is Mr. Burton. He is very hot and he is going to have tea with us, and he wrote those impressions in the Piccadilly Gazette which you gave me to read. My father is an Oriental scholar, Mr. Burton, but he is also interested in modern things."

Burton held out his hand.

"I try to understand London," he said. "It is enough for me. I know nothing about Assyria."

Mr. Cowper was a picturesque-looking old gentleman, with kind blue eyes and long white hair.

"It is quite natural," he assented. "You were born in London, without a doubt, you have lived there all your days and you write as one who sees. I was born in a library. I saw no city till I entered college. I had fashioned cities for myself long before then, and dwelt in them."

The girl had taken her place at the tea-table. Burton's eyes followed her admiringly.

"You were brought up in the country?" he asked his host.

"I was born in the City of Strange Imaginings," Mr. Cowper replied. "I read and read until I had learned the real art of fancy. No one who has ever learned it needs to look elsewhere for a dwelling house. It is the realism of your writing which fascinates me so, Mr. Burton. I wish you would stay here and write of my garden; the moorland, too, is beautiful."

"I should like to very much," said Burton.

Mr. Cowper gazed at him in mild curiosity.

"You are a stranger to me, Mr. Burton," he remarked. "My daughter does not often encourage visitors. Pray tell me, how did you make her acquaintance?" "There was a bull," he commenced,—"A cow," she interrupted softly.

"On the moor outside. Your daughter was a little terrified. She accepted my escort after I had driven away the—animal."

The old gentleman looked as though he thought it the most natural thing in the world.

"Dear me," he said, "how interesting! Edith, the strawberries this afternoon are delicious. You must show Mr.—Mr. Burton our kitchen gardens. Our south wall is famous."

This was the whole miracle of how Alfred Burton, whose first appearance in the neighborhood had been as an extremely objectionable tripper, was accepted almost as one of the family in a most exclusive little household. Edith, cool and graceful, sitting back in her wicker chair behind the daintily laid tea-table, seemed to take it all for granted. Mr. Cowper, after rambling on for some time, made an excuse and departed through the French windows of his library. Afterwards, Burton walked with his young hostess in the old-fashioned walled garden.

She treated him with the easy informality of privileged intimacy. She had accepted him as belonging, notwithstanding his damaging statements as to his antecedents, and he walked by the side of his divinity without a trace of awkwardness or nervousness. This world of Truth was indeed a world of easy ways! . . . The garden was fragrant with perfumes; the perfume of full-blown roses—great pink and yellow and white blossoms, drooping in clusters from trees and bushes; of lavender from an ancient bed; of stocks—pink and purple; of sweetbriar, growing in a hedge beyond. They walked aimlessly about along the gravel paths and across the deep greensward, and Burton knew no world, nor thought of any, save the world of that garden. But the girl, when they reached the boundary, leaned over the iron gate and her eyes were fixed northwards. It was the old story—she sighed for life and he for beauty. The walls of her prison-house were beautiful things, but not even the lichen and the moss and the peaches which already hung amber and red behind the thick leaves could ever make her wholly forget that they were, in a sense, symbolical—the walls of her life.

"To live here," he murmured, "must be like living in Paradise!"

She sighed. There was a little wistful droop about her lips; her eyes were still fixed northwards.

"I should like," he said, "to tell you a fairy story. It is about a wife and a little boy."

"Whose wife?" she asked quickly.

"Mine," he replied.

There was a brief silence. A shadow had passed across her face. She was very young and really very unsophisticated, and it may be that already the idea had presented itself, however faintly, that his might be the voice to call her into the promised land. Certain it is that after that silence some glory seemed to have passed from the summer evening.

"It is a fairy story and yet it is true," he went on, almost humbly. "Somehow, no one will believe it. Will you try?"

"I will try," she promised.

AFTERWARDS, HE HELD THE TWO beans in the palm of his hand and she turned them over curiously.

"Tell me again what your wife is like?" she asked.

He told her the pitiless truth and then there was a long silence. As he stood before her, a little breath of wind passed over the garden. He came back from the world of sordid places to the land of enchantment. There was certainly some spell upon him. He had found his way into a garden which lay beyond the world. He was conscious all at once of a strange mixture of spicy perfumes, a faint sense of intoxication, of weird, delicate emotions which caught at the breath in his throat and sent the blood dancing through his veins, warmed to a new and wonderful music. Her blue eyes were a little dimmed, the droop of her head a little sad. Quite close to them was a thick bed of lavender. He looked at the beans in his hand and his eyes sought the thickest part of the clustering mass of foliage and blossom. She had lifted her eyes now and it seemed to him that she had divined his purpose—approved of it, even. Her slim, white-clad body swayed towards him. She appeared to have abandoned finally the faint aloofness of her attitude. He raised his hand. Then she stopped him. The moment, whatever its dangers may have been, had passed.

"I do not know whether your story is an allegory or not," she said softly. "It really doesn't matter, does it? You must come and see me again—afterwards."

X

No Reconciliation

Burton travelled down to Garden Green on the following morning by the Tube, which he hated, and walked along the familiar avenue with loathing at his heart. There was no doubt about Ellen's being at home. The few feet of back yard were full of white garments of unlovely shape, recently washed and fluttering in the breeze. The very atmosphere was full of soapsuds. Ellen herself opened the door to him, her skirts pinned up around her, and a clothes-peg in her mouth.

He greeted her with an effort at pleasantness. "Good morning, Ellen," he said. "I am glad to find you at home. May I come in?"

Ellen removed the clothes-peg from her mouth.

"It's your own house, isn't it?" she replied, with a suspicious little quiver in her tone. "I don't suppose you've forgotten your way into the parlor. Keep well away from me or you may get some soapsuds on your fine clothes."

She raised her red arms above her head and flattened herself against the wall with elaborate care. Burton, hating himself and the whole situation, stepped into the parlor. Ellen followed him as far as the threshold.

"What is it you want?" she demanded, still retaining one foot in the passage. "I'm busy. You haven't forgotten that it's Friday morning, have you?"

"I want to talk to you for a little while," he said, gently. "I have something to propose which may improve our relations."

Ellen's attitude became one of fierce contempt mingled with a slight tremulousness.

"Such ridiculous goings-on and ways of speaking!" she muttered. "Well, if you've anything to say to me you'll have to wait a bit, that's all. I've got some clothes I can't leave all in a scurry like this. I'll send Alf in to keep you company."

Burton sighed but accepted his fate. For a few moments he sat upon the sofa and gazed around at the hopeless little room. Then, in due course, the door was pushed open and Alfred appeared, his hair shiny, his cheeks redolent of recent ablutions, more than a trifle reluctant. His conversation was limited to a few monosyllables and a whoop of joy at the receipt of a shilling. His efforts at escape afterwards were so pitiful that Burton eventually let him out of the window, from which he disappeared, running at full tilt towards a confectioner's shop.

Presently Ellen returned. It was exceedingly manifest that her temporary absence had not been wholly due to the exigencies of her domestic occupation. Her skirt was unpinned, a mauve bow adorned her throat, a scarf of some gauzy material, also mauve, floated around her neck. She was wearing a hat with a wing, which he was guiltily conscious of having once admired, and which she attempted, in an airy but exceedingly unconvincing fashion, to explain.

"Got to go up the street directly," she said, jerkily. "What is it?"

Burton had made up his mind that the fewer words he employed, the better.

"Ellen," he began, "you have perhaps noticed a certain change in me during the last few weeks?"

Ellen's bosom began to heave and her eyes to flash. Burton hastened on.

"You will find it hard to believe how it all occurred," he continued. "I want you to, though, if you can. There have been many instances of diet influencing morals, but none quite—"

"Diet doing what?" Ellen broke in. "What's that?" Burton came very straight to the point.

"This change in me," he explained simply, "is merely because I have taken something which makes it impossible for me to say or see anything but the absolute truth. I could not tell you a falsehood if I tried. Wherever I look, or whenever I listen, I can always see or hear truth. I know nothing about music, yet since this thing happened it has been a wonderful joy to me. I can tell a false note in a second, I can tell true music from false. I know nothing about art, yet I can suddenly feel it and all its marvels. You can understand a little, perhaps, what this means? A whole new world, full of beautiful objects and inspirations, has suddenly come into my life."

Ellen stared at him blankly.

"Have you gone dotty, Alfred?" she murmured.

He shook his head.

"No," he replied gently. "If anything, I am a great deal wiser than ever I was before. Only there are penalties. It is about these penalties that I want to talk to you."

Ellen's arms became crooked and her knuckles were screwed into her waist. It was an unfortunate and inherited habit of hers, which reappeared frequently under circumstances of emotion.

"Will you answer this one question?" she insisted. "Why has all this made you leave your wife and home? Tell me that, will you?"

Burton went for his last fence gallantly.

"Because our life here is hideous," he declared, "and I can't stand it. Our house is ugly, our furniture impossible, the neighborhood atrocious. Your clothes are all wrong and so are Alfred's. I could not possibly live here any longer in the way we have been living up to now."

Ellen gave a little gasp.

"Then what are you doing here now?"

"I cannot come back to you," he continued. "I want you to come to me. This is the part of my story which will sound miraculous, if not ridiculous to you, but you will have to take my word for it. Try and remember for a moment that there are things in life beyond the pale of our knowledge, things which we must accept simply by faith. The change which came to me came through eating a sort of bean, grown by an old man who was brought home from Asia by a great scholar. These beans are supposed to contain the germ of Truth. I have 'two here—one for you and one for Alfred. I want you to eat them, and afterwards, what I hope and believe is that we shall see things more the same way and come together again."

He produced the beans from his pocket and Ellen took a step forward. The shortness of her breath and the glitter in her eyes should have warned him. The greatness of his subject, however, had carried him away. His attention was riveted upon the beans lying in the palm of his hand. He looked at them almost reverently.

"Are those the things?" she demanded.

He held them out towards her. A faint pang of regret stirred his heart. For a single second the picture of a beautiful garden glowed and faded before his eyes. A wave of delicious perfume came and went. The girl— slim, white-clad—looked at him a little wistfully with her sad blue eyes. It was a mirage which passed, a mirage or some dear, vanishing dream.

"Take one yourself, Ellen," he directed. "Keep the other one carefully for Alfred."

She snatched them from his hand and before he could stop her she had thrown them out of the open window into the street. He was, for an instant, stricken dumb.

"And you," she cried fiercely, "you can follow your—beans, as soon as you choose!"

He looked at her and realized how completely he had failed. She was indeed stirred to the very depths of her nature, but the emotion which possessed her was one of passionate and jealous anger.

"Not good enough for you as we are, eh?" she cried. "You don't like our clothes or our manners! You've got to be a fine gentleman in five minutes, haven't you? We were good enough for you when thirty shillings a week didn't seem enough to keep us out of debt, and I stitched my fingers to the bone with odd bits of dressmaking. Good enough for you then, my man, when I cooked your dinner, washed your clothes, kept your house clean and bore your son, working to the last moment till my head swam and my knees tottered. Truth! Truth, indeed! What is there but truth in my life, I'd like to know? Have I ever told you a lie? Have I ever looked at another man, or let one touch my fingers, since the day when you put that ring on? And now—take it—and get out!"

She wrenched her wedding ring from her finger and threw it upon the ground between them. Her bosom was heaving; her cheeks were red and her eyes glittering. Several wisps of her hair had been unable to stand the excitement and were hanging down. The mauve bow had worked its way on to one side—very nearly under her ear. There was no deceit nor any pretence about her. She was the daughter of a washerwoman and a greengrocer, and heredity had triumphantly asserted itself. Yet as he backed towards the door before her fierce onslaught, Burton, for the first time since this new thing had come, positively admired her.

"Ellen," he protested, "you are behaving foolishly. I wanted you and the boy to understand. I wanted you to share the things which I had found. It was the only way we could be happy together."

"Alfred and I will look after ourselves and our own happiness," she declared, with a little gulp.

"Other women have lost their husbands. I can bear it. Why don't you go? Don't you know the way out?"

Burton offered his hand. She frankly scoffed at him.

"I don't understand all that rigmarole about truth," she concluded, "but I'm no sort of a one at pretense. Outside, my man, and stay outside!"

She slammed the door. Burton found himself in the street. Instinctively he felt that her hasty dismissal was intended to conceal from him the torrent of tears which were imminent. A little dazed, he still groped his way to the spot where Ellen had thrown the beans. A man was there with a fruit barrow, busy, apparently, rearranging his stock. Something about his appearance struck Burton with a chill premonition. He came to a standstill and looked at him.

"Did you wish to buy any fruit, sir?" the man asked, in a tone unusually subdued for one of his class.

Burton shook his head.

"I was just wondering what you were doing," he remarked.

The man hesitated.

"To tell you the truth, guvnor," he confessed, "I was mixing up my apples and bananas a bit. You see, those at the top were all the best, and it has been my custom to add a few from underneath there—most of them a little going off. It was the only way," he added with a sigh, "that one could make a profit. I have made up my mind, though, to either throw them away or sell them separately for what they are worth, which isn't much. I've had enough of deceiving the public. If I can't get a living honestly with this barrow, I'll try another job."

"Do you happen to have eaten anything just lately?" Burton asked him, with a sinking heart.

The man looked at his questioner, for a moment, doubtfully.

"'Ad my breakfast at seven," he replied. "Just a bite of bread and cheese since, with my morning beer."

"Nothing since—not anything at all?" Burton pressed.

"I picked up a funny-colored bean and ate it, a few minutes ago. Queer flavor it had, too. Nothing else that I can think of."

Burton looked at the man and down at his barrow. He glanced around at the neighborhood in which he had to make a living. Then he groaned softly to himself.

"Good luck to you!" he murmured, and turned away.

XI

The Gate into Paradise

The girl looked up from her seat wonderingly. His coming had been a little precipitate. His appearance, too, betokened a disturbed mind. "There is a front door," she reminded him. "There are also bells."

"I could not wait," he answered simply. "I saw the flutter of your gown as I came along the lane, and I climbed the wall. All the way down I fancied that you might be wearing blue."

A slight air of reserve which she had carefully prepared for him, faded away. What was the use? He was such an extraordinary person! It was not possible to measure him by the usual standards. She was obliged to smile.

"You find blue—becoming?"

"Adorable," he replied, fervently. "I have dreamed of you in blue. You wore blue only the night before last, when I wrote my little sketch of 'The Pavements of Bond Street on a Summer Afternoon.'"

She pointed to the journal which lay at her feet.

"I recognized myself, of course," she declared, trying to speak severely. "It was most improper of you."

"It was nothing of the sort," he answered bluntly. "You came into the picture and I could not keep you out. You were there, so you had to stay."

"It was much too flattering," she objected.

Again he contradicted her.

"I could not flatter if I tried," he assured her. "It was just you."

She laughed softly.

"It is so difficult to argue with you," she murmured. "All the same, I think that it was most improper. But then everything you do is improper. You had no right to climb over that wall, you had no right to walk here with me the other afternoon, even though you had driven away a tame cow. You have no right whatever to be here to-day. What about your wife?"

"I have been to Garden Green," he announced. "I offered her emancipation, the same emancipation as that which I myself have attained. She refused it absolutely. She is satisfied with Garden Green."

"You mean," the girl asked, "that she refuses the—the—"

"Beans," he said. "Precisely! She did more than refuse them—she threw them out of the window. She has no imagination. From her point of view I suppose she behaved in a perfectly natural fashion. She told me to go my own way and leave her alone."

Edith sighed.

"It is very unfortunate," she declared, "that you were not able to convince her."

"Is it?" he replied. "I tried my best, and when I had failed I was glad."

She raised her eyes for a moment but she shook her head.

"I am afraid that it doesn't make any difference, does it?"

"Why not? It makes all the difference," he insisted.

"My dear Mr. Burton," she expostulated, making room for him to sit down beside her, "I cannot possibly allow you to make love to me because your wife refuses to swallow a bean!"

"But she threw them out of the window!" he persisted. "She understood quite well what she was doing. Her action was entirely symbolical. She declared for Garden Green and the vulgar life."

For a girl who lived in an old-fashioned garden, and who seemed herself to be part of a fairy story, Edith certainly took a practical view of the situation.

"I am afraid," she murmured, "that the Divorce Courts have no jurisdiction over your case. You are therefore a married man, and likely to continue a married man. I cannot possibly allow you to hold my hand."

His head swam for a moment. She was very alluring with her pale face set in its clouds of golden hair, her faintly wrinkled forehead, her bewitchingly regretful smile—regretful, yet in a sense provocative.

"I am in love with you," he declared.

"Naturally," she replied. "The question is—" She paused and looked intently at the tip of her slipper. It was very small and very pointed and it was quite impossible to ignore the fact that she had a remarkably pretty foot and that she wore white silk stockings. Burton had never known any one before who wore white silk stockings.

"I am very much in love with you," he repeated. "I cannot help it. It is not my fault—that is to say, it is as much your fault as it is mine."

The corners of her mouth twitched.

"Is it? Well, what are you going to do about it?"

"I am going to take you down to the orchard, through the little gate, and across the plank into the hayfield," he announced, boldly. "I am going to sit with you under the oak tree, where we can just catch the view of the moor through the dip in the hills. We will lean back and watch the clouds—those little white, fleecy, broken-off pieces—and I will tell you fairy stories. We shall be quite alone there and perhaps you will let me hold your hand."

She shook her head, gently but very firmly. "Such things are impossible."

"Because I have a wife at Garden Green?"

She nodded.

"Because you have a wife, and because—I had really quite forgotten to mention it before, but as a matter of fact I am half engaged to someone myself."

He went suddenly white.

"You are not serious?" he demanded. "Perfectly," she assured him. "I can't think how I forgot it."

"Does he come here to see you?" Burton asked, jealously.

"Not very often. He has to work hard." Burton leaned back in his seat. The music of life seemed suddenly to be playing afar off—so far that he could only dimly catch the strains. The wind, too, must have changed—the perfume of the roses reached him no more.

"I thought you understood," he said slowly.

She did not speak again for several moments. Then she rose a little abruptly to her feet.

"You can walk as far as the hayfield with me," she said.

They passed down the narrow garden path in single file. There had been a storm in the night and the beds of pink and white stocks lay dashed and drooping with a weight of glistening rain-drops. The path was strewn with rose petals and the air seemed fuller than ever of a fresh and delicate fragrance. At the end of the garden, a little gate led into the orchard. Side by side they passed beneath the trees.

"Tell me," he begged in a low tone, "about this lover of yours!"

"There is so little to tell," she answered. "He is a member of the firm who publish books for my father. He is quite kind to us both. He used to come down here more often, even, than he does now, and one night he asked my father whether he might speak to me."

"And your father?"

"My father was very much pleased," she continued. "We have little money and father is not very strong. He told me that it had taken a weight off his mind."

"How often does he come?" Burton asked.

"He was here last Sunday week."

"Last Sunday week! And you call him your lover!"

"No, I have not called him that," she reminded him gently. "He is not that sort of man. Only I think that he is the person whom I shall marry—some day."

"I am sure that you were beginning to like me," he insisted.

She turned and looked at him—at his pale, eager face with the hollow eyes, the tremulous mouth—a curiously negative and wholly indescribable figure, yet in some dim sense impressive through certain unspelt suggestions of latent force. No one could have described him, in those days, though no one with perceptions could have failed to observe much that was unusual in his personality.

"It is true," she admitted. "I do like you. You seem to carry some quality with you which I do not understand. What is it, I wonder? It is something which reminds me of your writing."

"I think that it is truthfulness," he told her. "That is no virtue on my part. It is sheer necessity. I am quite sure that if I had not been obliged I should never have told you that it was I who stared at you from the Common there, one of a hideous little band of trippers. I should not even have told you about my wife. It is all so humiliating."

"It was yourself which obliged yourself," she pointed out,—"I mean that the truthfulness was part of yourself. Do you know, it has set me thinking so often. If only people realized how attractive absolute simplicity, absolute candor is, the world would be so much easier a place to live in, and so much more beautiful! Life is so full of small shams, so many imperfectly hidden little deceits. Even if you had not told me this strange story about yourself, I think that I should still have felt this quality about you."

"I should like," he declared, "to have you conceive a passion for the truth. I should like to have you feel that it was not possible to live anyhow or anywhere else save in its light. If you really felt that it would be like a guiding star to you through life, you would never be able even to consider marriage with a man whom you did not love."

"This evening," she said slowly, "he is coming down. I was thinking it all over this afternoon. I had made up my mind to say nothing about you. Since you came, however, I feel differently. I shall tell him everything."

"Perhaps," Burton suggested, hopefully, "he may be jealous."

"It is possible," she assented. "He does not seem like that but one can never tell."

"He may even give you up!"

She smiled.

"If he did," she reminded him, "it would not make any difference."

"I will not admit that," he declared. "I want your love—I want your whole love. I want you to feel the same things that I feel, in the same way. You live in two places—in a real garden and a fairy garden, the fairy garden of my dreams. I want you to leave the real garden and let me try and teach you how beautiful the garden of fancies may become."

She sighed.

"Alas!" she said, "it is because I may not come and live always in that fairy garden that I am going to send you away."

"Don't!" he pleaded,—"not altogether, at any rate. Life is so short, so pitifully incomplete. We live through so many epochs and each epoch has its own personality. It was not I who married Ellen. It was Burton, the auctioneer's clerk. I cannot carry the burden of that fellow's asinine mistakes upon my shoulders forever."

"I am afraid," she murmured, "that however clever the Mr. Burton of to-day may be, he will never be able to rid himself altogether of his predecessor's burdens."

They were leaning over the gate, looking into the deserted hayfield. The quiet of evening had stolen down upon them. He drew a little nearer to her.

"Dear," he whispered, "there isn't really any Ellen, there isn't really any woman in the world of my thoughts, the world in which I live, save you."

She was almost in his arms. She did not resist but she looked a little pitifully into his face. "You will not—please!" she begged.

Once more the music passed away into the clouds. It was the gate into Paradise over which he had leaned, but the gate was locked, and as he stood there it seemed to grow higher and higher, until he could not even see over the top. Almost roughly he turned away.

"Quite right," he muttered. "I must not touch the Princess of my fairy garden. Only let us go back now, please. I cannot stay here any longer."

She obeyed at once. There was a queer, pathetic little droop at the corners of her lips, and she avoided his eyes.

"Good-bye!" he said.

His tone was dull and spiritless. Something, for the moment, seemed to have passed from him. He seemed, indeed, to lack both inspiration and courage. Her fingers clung slightly to his. She was praying, even, that he might laugh to scorn her unspoken appeal. He moved a yard away and stood looking at her. Her heart began to beat wildly. Surely her prayer would be granted! The light of adoration was coming back to his eyes.

"I cannot see the truth!" he cried hoarsely. "You belong to me—I feel that you belong to me! You are part of the great life. I have found you—you are mine! And yet. . . I feel I mustn't touch you. I don't understand. Perhaps I shall come back."

He turned and hurried off. She watched him until he was a speck upon the road; watched him, even then, from among the shadows of the trees. There was a lump in her throat and a misty light in her eyes. She had forgotten everything that had seemed absurd to her in this strange little romance. Her eyes and her arms, almost her lips, were calling him to her.

XII

A Bolt from the Blue

Burton's life moved for a time among the easy places. The sub-editor of the Piccadilly Gazette, to which he still contributed, voluntarily increased his scale of pay and was insatiable in his demand for copy. Burton moved into pleasant rooms in a sunny corner of an old-fashioned square. He sent Ellen three pounds a week—all she would accept—and save for a dull pain at his heart which seldom left him, he found much pleasure in life. Then came the first little break in the clear sky. Mr. Waddington came in to see him one day and Mr. Waddington was looking distinctly worried. He was neatly and tastefully dressed, and his demeanor had lost all its old offensiveness. His manner, too, was immensely improved. His tone was almost gentle. Nevertheless, there was a perplexed frown upon his forehead and an anxious look in his eyes.

"Business all right, I hope?" Burton asked him, after he had welcomed his late employer, installed him in an easy chair and pushed a box of cigarettes towards him.

"It is better than all right," Mr. Waddington replied. "It is wonderful. We have never had such crowds at the sales, and I have taken on four more clerks in the house-letting department."

Burton laughed softly. The humor of the auctioneer's position appealed to him immensely.

"I am making money fast," Mr. Waddington admitted, without enthusiasm. "Another year or two of this and I could retire comfortably."

"Then what," Burton asked, "is the worry?"

Mr. Waddington smoked vigorously for a moment. "Has it ever occurred to you, Burton," he inquired, "to ask yourself whether this peculiar state, in which you and I find ourselves, may be wholly permanent?"

Burton was genuinely startled. He sat looking at his visitor like one turned to stone. The prospect called up by that simple question was appalling. His cigarette burned idly away between his fingers. The shadow of fear lurked in his eyes.

"Not permanent?" he repeated. "I never thought of that. Why do you ask?"

Mr. Waddington scratched his chin thoughtfully. It was not a graceful proceeding, and Burton, with a sinking heart, remembered that this was one of his employer's old habits. He scrutinized his visitor more closely. Although his appearance at first sight was immaculate, there were certain alarming symptoms to be noted. His linen collar was certainly doing service for the second time, and Burton noticed with dismay a slight revival of the auctioneer's taste for loud colors in his shirt and socks.

"It was yesterday afternoon," Mr. Waddington continued. "I was selling an oak chest. I explained that it was not a genuine antique but that it had certainly some claims to antiquity on account of its design. That seemed to me to be a very fair way of putting it. Then I saw a man, who was very keen on buying it, examining the brass handles. He looked up at me. 'Why, the handles are genuine!' he exclaimed. 'They're real old brass, anyway!' Now I knew quite well, Burton, that those handles, though they were extraordinarily near the real thing, were not genuine. I opened my mouth to tell him so, and then, Burton, do you know that I hesitated?"

"You didn't tell him—that they were genuine!" Burton gasped.

Mr. Waddington shook his head.

"No," he admitted, "I did not go so far as that. Still, it was almost as great a shock to me. I felt a distinct impulse to tell him that they were. A few days ago, such an idea would never have entered my head. It would have been a sheer impossibility."

"Anything else?"

Mr. Waddington hesitated. He seemed to be feeling the shame of these avowals.

"This morning," he confessed, "I passed the door of the Golden Lion on my way to the office. For the first time since—you know when—I felt a desire—a faint desire but still it was there—to go in and chaff Milly and have a pint of beer in a tankard. I didn't go, of course, but I felt the impulse, nevertheless."

Burton had turned very pale.

"This," he exclaimed, "is terrible! What have you done with the rest of the beans?"

"I have nine," Mr. Waddington replied. "I carry them in my waistcoat pocket. I am perfectly convinced now that there is trouble ahead, for on my way up the stairs here I felt a strong inclination to tell you that I had lost them, in case you should want any."

"It would be only fair," Burton declared warmly, "to divide them." Mr. Waddington frowned.

"I SEE NO REASON FOR that at all," he objected, feeling his waistcoat pocket. "The beans are in my possession."

"But if we are to revert to our former state of barbarism," Burton urged, "let us at least do so together."

"You are some time ahead of me," Mr. Waddington pointed out. "None of these warnings have come to you yet. It may be something wrong with my disposition, or the way I have swallowed my bean. Yours may be a permanent affair."

Burton hesitated. Then he threw himself into a chair and buried his face in his hands.

"My time is coming, too!" he confessed mournfully. "I am in the same position. Even while you were speaking just now, I felt a strong desire to deceive you, to invent some experience similar to your own."

"Are you sure of that?" Mr. Waddington asked anxiously.

"Quite sure!" Burton groaned.

"Then we are both of us in it, and that's a fact," Mr. Waddington affirmed.

Burton looked up.

"About those beans?"

Mr. Waddington thought for some few moments.

"I shall keep five and give you four," he decided. "It is treating you very generously. I am not obliged to give you any at all, you know. I am doing it because I am good-natured and because we are in this thing together. If the worst happens, you can come back to your old place in the firm. I dare say we shall pull along somehow."

Burton shuddered from head to foot. He saw it all mapped out before him—the miserable routine of dull, undignified work, the whole intolerable outlook of that daily life. He covered his face with his hands to shut out the prospect.

"I couldn't come back!" he muttered "I couldn't!"

"That's all very well," Mr. Waddington objected, "but if this thing really passes off, you'll be only too glad to. I suppose I shall flirt with Milly again, and drink beer, give up Ruskin for the Sporting Times, wear loud clothes, tell most frightful falsehoods when I sell that terrible furniture and buy another trotting horse to drive out on Sundays. Oh, Lord!"

Mr. Waddington rose slowly to his feet. He lit a cigarette, sniffed it, and looked at it disparagingly. It was very fine Turkish tobacco and one of Burton's extravagances.

"I am not sure, after all," he declared, "that there isn't more flavor in a British cigar."

Burton shuddered

"You had better take a bean at once," he groaned. "Those cigarettes are made from the finest tobacco imported."

Mr. Waddington felt in his waistcoat pocket with trembling fingers, slowly produced a little silver box, took out a bean and crunched it between his teeth. An expression of immense relief at once spread over his features. He sniffed at his cigarette with an air of keen appreciation, and deliberately handed over to Burton his share of the remaining beans.

"I am myself again," he declared firmly. "I can feel the change already."

Burton eyed him anxiously.

"Cigarette taste all right now?"

"Delicious!" Mr. Waddington replied. "Most exquisite tobacco! Makes me shiver inside to think how I could ever have smoked that other filthy rubbish."

"No idea of calling in at the Golden Lion on your way back, eh?" Burton persisted.

Mr. Waddington's expression was full of reproach. "The very thought of that place, with its smell of stale beer and those awful creatures behind the bar, makes me shiver," he confessed. "I shall walk for an hour before lunch in Kensington Gardens. If I have a moment to spare I shall run into the Museum and spend a little time with the mosaics. What a charming effect the sunlight has coming through those trees, Burton! I want you to come down and see my rooms sometime. I have picked up a few trifles that I think you would appreciate."

"I will come with pleasure," Burton replied. "This afternoon, if you could spare a few minutes?" the auctioneer suggested. "We might go around and look at that Romney which has just been unearthed. I have been to Christie's three times already to see it, but I should like to take you. There's something about the face which I don't quite understand. There is a landscape there, too, just sent up from some country house, which I think would interest you."

Burton shook his head and moved feverishly towards his desk.

"I am going to work," he declared. "You have frightened me a little. I must economize time. I shall write a novel, a novel of real life. I must write it while I can still see the perfect truth."

XIII

PROOF POSITIVE

Burton did not get very far with his novel. About nine o'clock on the same evening, Mr. Waddington, who was spending a quiet hour or two with his books, was disturbed by a hasty knock at the door of his rooms. He rose with some reluctance from his chair to answer the summons.

"Burton!" he exclaimed.

Burton came quickly in. He was paler, even, than usual, and there were black shadows under his eyes. There was a change in his face, indescribable but very apparent. His eyes had lost their dreamy look, he glanced furtively about him, he had the air of a man who has committed a crime and fears detection. His dress was not nearly so neat as usual. Mr. Waddington, whose bachelor evening clothes—a loose dinner-jacket and carefully tied black tie—were exactly as they should be, glanced disparagingly at his visitor.

"My dear Burton," he gasped, "whatever is the matter with you? You seem all knocked over."

Burton had thrown himself into a chair. He was contemplating the little silver box which he had drawn from his pocket.

"I've got to take one of these," he muttered, "that's all. When I have eaten it, there will be three left. I took the last one exactly two months and four days ago. At the same rate, in just eight months and sixteen days I shall be back again in bondage."

Mr. Waddington was very much interested. He was also a little distressed.

"Are you quite sure," he asked, "of your symptoms?"

"Absolutely certain," Burton declared sadly. "I found myself this evening trying to kiss my landlady's daughter, who is not in the least good-looking. I was attracted by the programme of a music hall and had hard work to keep from going there. A man asked me the way to Leicester Square just now, and I almost directed him wrongly for the sheer pleasure of telling a lie. I nearly bought some ties at an outfitter's shop in the Strand—such ties! It's awful—awful, Mr. Waddington!"

Mr. Waddingon nodded his head compassionately.

"I suppose you know what you're talking about," he said. "You see, I have already taken my second bean and to me the things that you have spoken of seem altogether incredible. I could not bring myself to believe that an absolute return to those former horrible conditions would be possible for either you or me. By the bye," he added, with a sudden change of tone, "I've just managed to get a photograph of the Romney I was telling you of."

Burton waved it away.

"It doesn't interest me in the least," he declared gloomily. "I very nearly bought a copy of Ally Sloper on my way down here."

Mr. Waddington shivered.

"I suppose there is no hope for you," he said. "It is excessively painful for me to see you in this state. On the whole, I think that the sooner you take the bean, the better."

Burton suddenly sat up in his chair.

"What are those sheets of paper you have on the table?" he asked quickly.

"They are the sheets of paper left with the little flower-pot in the room of Idlemay House," Mr. Waddington answered. "I was just looking them through and wondering what language it was they were written in. It is curious, too, that our friend should have only translated the last few lines."

Burton rose from his chair and leaned over the table, looking at them with keen interest.

"It was about those papers that I started out to come and see you," he declared. "There must be some way by which we could make the action of these beans more permanent. I propose that we get the rest of the pages translated. We may find them most valuable."

Mr. Waddington was rather inclined to favor the idea.

"I cannot think," he admitted, "why it never occurred to us before. Whom do you propose to take them to?"

"There is some one I know who lives a little way down in the country," Burton replied. "He is a great antiquarian and Egyptologist, and if any one can translate them, I should think he would be able to. Lend me the sheets of manuscript just as they are, and I will take them down to him to-morrow. It may tell us, perhaps, how to deal with the plant so that we can get more of the beans. Eight months is no use to me. When I am like this, just drifting back, everything seems possible. I can even see myself back at Clematis Villa, walking with Ellen, listening to the band, leaning over the bar of the Golden Lion. Listen!"

He stopped short. A barrel organ outside was playing a music hall ditty. His head kept time to the music.

"I wish I had my banjo!" he exclaimed, impulsively. Then he shivered. "Did you hear that? A banjo! I used to play it, you know."

Mr. Waddington looked shocked.

"The banjo!" he repeated. "Do you really mean that you want to play it at the present moment?"

"I do," Burton replied. "If I had it with me now, I should play that tune. I should play others like it. Everything seems to be slipping away from me. I can smell the supper cooking in my little kitchen at Clematis Villa. Delicious! My God, I can't bear it any longer! Here goes!"

He took a bean from his pocket with trembling fingers and swallowed it. Then he leaned back in his chair for several moments with closed eyes. When he opened them again, an expression of intense relief was upon his face.

"I am coming back already," he declared faintly. "Thank Heavens! Mr. Waddington, your room is charming, sir. Japanese prints, too! I had no idea that you were interested in them. That third one is exquisite. And what a dado!"

"Hewlings himself designed it for me," Mr. Waddington observed, with satisfaction. "There are several things I should like you to notice, Burton. That lacquer-work box!"

Burton was already holding it in his fingers and was gazing at it lovingly.

"It is perfect," he admitted. "What workmanship! You are indeed fortunate, Mr. Waddington. And isn't that Mona Lisa on the walls? What a beautiful reproduction! I am saving up money even now to go to Paris to see the original. Only a few nights ago I was reading Pater's appreciation of it."

He rose and wandered around the room, making murmured comments all the time. Presently he came back to the table and glanced down at the sheets of manuscript.

"Mr. Waddington," he said, "let me take these to my friend. I feel that the last few hours must have been a sort of nightmare, and yet—"

He drew out a little box from his waistcoat pocket and peered inside. He was suddenly grave.

"It was no nightmare, then," he muttered. "I have really taken a bean."

E. PHILLIPS OPPENHEIM

"You took it not a quarter of an hour ago," Mr. Waddington told him.

Burton sighed.

"It is awful to imagine that I should have needed it," he confessed. "There must be some way out of this. You will trust me with these sheets, Mr. Waddington? If my friend in the country can do nothing for us, I will take them to the British Museum."

"By all means," Mr. Waddington replied. "Take care of them and bring them back safely. I should like, if possible, to have a written translation. It should indeed prove most interesting."

Burton went out with the musky-smelling sheets in his pocket. All the temptations of the earlier part of the evening had completely passed away. He walked slowly because a big yellow moon hung down from the sky, and because Mr. Waddington's rooms were in a neighborhood of leafy squares and picturesque houses. When he came back to the more travelled ways he ceased, however, to look about him. He took a 'bus to Westminster and returned to his rooms. Somehow or other, the possession of the sheets acted like a sedative. He felt a new confidence in himself. The absurdity of any return to his former state had never been more established. The remainder of the night he spent in the same way as many others. He drew his writing-table up to the open window, and with the lights of the city and the river spread out before him, and the faint wind blowing into the room, he worked at his novel.

XIV

The Legend of the Perfect Food

A foretaste of autumn had crept into the midst of summer. There were gray clouds in the sky, a north wind booming across the moors. Burton even shivered as he walked down the hill to the house where she lived. There was still gorse, still heather, still a few roses in the garden and a glimmering vision of the beds of other flowers in the background. But the sun which gave them life was hidden. Burton looked eagerly into the garden and his heart sank. There was no sign there of any living person. After a moment's hesitation, he opened the gate, passed up the neat little path and rang the bell. It was opened after the briefest of delays by the trim parlor-maid.

"Is your mistress at home?" he asked.

"Miss Edith has gone to London for two days, sir," the girl announced. "The professor is in his study, sir."

Burton stood quite still for a moment. It was absurd that his heart should be so suddenly heavy, that all the spring and buoyancy should have gone out of life! For the first time he realized the direction in which his thoughts had been travelling since he had left his rooms an hour ago. He had to remind himself that it was the professor whom he had come to see.

Mr. Cowper received him graciously, if a little vaguely. Burton wasted no time, however, in announcing the nature of his errand. Directly he produced the sheets, the professor became interested. The faint odor which seemed shaken out from them into the room stimulated his curiosity. He sniffed at it with great content.

"Strange," he remarked, "very strange. I haven't smelt that perfume since I was with the excavators at Chaldea. A real Oriental flavor, young man, about your manuscript."

"There is very little of it," Burton said,—"just a page or so which apparently the writer never had time to finish. The sheets came into my hands in rather a curious way, and I should very much like to have an exact translation of them. I don't even know what the language is. I thought, perhaps, that you might be able to help me. I will explain to you later, if you will allow me, the exact nature of my interest in them."

Mr. Cowper took the pages into his hand with a benevolent smile. At the first glance, however, his expression changed. It was obvious that he was greatly interested. It was obvious, also, that he was correspondingly surprised.

"My dear young man," he exclaimed, "my dear Mr.—Mr. Burton— why, this is wonderful! Where did you get these sheets, do you say? Are you honestly telling me that they were written within the last thousand years?"

"Without a doubt," Burton replied. "They were written in London, a few months ago."

Mr. Cowper was already busy surrounding himself with strange-looking volumes. His face displayed the utmost enthusiasm in his task.

"It is most amazing, this," he declared, drawing a chair up to the table. "These sheets are written in a language which has been dead as a medium of actual intercourse for over two thousand years. You meet with it sometimes in old Egyptian manuscripts. There was a monastery somewhere near the excavations which I had the honor to conduct in Syria, where an ancient prayer-book contained several prayers in this language. Literally I cannot translate this for you; actually I will. I can get at the sense—I can get at the sense quite well. But if one could only find the man who wrote it! He is the man I should like to see, Mr. Burton. If the pages were written so recently, where is the writer?"

"He is dead," Burton replied.

Mr. Cowper sighed.

"Well, well," he continued, starting upon his task with avidity, "we will talk about him presently. This is indeed miraculous. I am most grateful—deeply grateful to you—for having brought me this manuscript."

Mr. Cowper was busy for the next quarter of an hour. His expression, as he turned up dictionaries and made notes, was still full of the liveliest and most intense interest. Presently he leaned back in his chair. He kept one hand upon the loose sheets of manuscript, while with the other he removed his spectacles. Then he closed his eyes for a moment.

"My young friend," he said, "did you ever hear a quaint Asiatic legend—scarcely a legend, perhaps, but a superstition—that many and many a wise man, four thousand years ago, spent his nights and his days, not as our more modern scientists of a few hundred years ago have done, in the attempt to turn baser metals into gold, but in the attempt to constitute from simple elements the perfect food for man?"

Burton shook his head. He was somewhat mystified.

"I have never heard anything of the sort," he acknowledged.

"The whole literature of ancient Egypt and the neighboring countries," Mr. Cowper proceeded, "abounds with mystical stories of this perfect food. It was to come to man in the nature of a fruit. It was to give him, not eternal life—for that was valueless—but eternal and absolute understanding, so that nothing in life could be harmful, nothing save objects and thoughts of beauty could present themselves to the understanding of the fortunate person who partook of it. These pages which you have brought to me to translate are concerned with this superstition. The writer claims here that after centuries of research and blending and grafting, carried on without a break by the priests of his family, each one handing down, together with an inheritance of his sacerdotal office, many wonderful truths respecting the growth of this fruit,—the writer of these lines claims here, that he, the last of his line, has succeeded in producing the one perfect food, from which everything gross is eliminated, and whose spiritual result upon a normal man is such as to turn him from a thing of clay into something approaching a god."

"Does he mention anything about beans?" Burton asked anxiously.

Mr. Cowper nodded benignantly.

"The perfect food referred to," he said, "appears to have been produced in the shape of small beans. They are to be eaten with great care, and to ensure permanency in the results, a green leaf of the little tree is to follow the consumption of the bean."

Burton sprang to his feet.

"A thousand thanks, professor!" he cried. "That is the one thing we were seeking to discover. The leaves, of course!"

Mr. Cowper looked at his visitor in amazement.

"My young friend," he said, "are you going to tell me that you have seen one of these beans?"

"Not only that but I have eaten one," Burton announced,—"in fact I have eaten two."

Mr. Cowper was greatly excited.

"Where are they?" he exclaimed. "Show me one! Where is the tree? How did the man come to write this? Where did he write it? Let me look at one of the beans!"

Burton produced the little silver snuff-box in which he carried them. With his left hand he kept the professor away.

"Mr. Cowper," he said, "I cannot let you touch them or handle them. They mean more to me than I can tell you, yet there they are. Look at them. And let me tell you this. That old superstition you have spoken of has truth in it. These beans are indeed a spiritual food. They alter character. They have the most amazing effect upon a man's moral system."

"Young man," Mr. Cowper insisted, "I must eat one."

Burton shook his head.

"Mr. Cowper," he said, "there are reasons why I find it very hard to deny you anything, but as regards those three beans, you will neither eat one nor even hold it in your hand. Sit down and I will tell you a story which sounds as though it might have happened a thousand years ago. It happened within the last three months. Listen."

Burton told his story with absolute sincerity. The professor listened with intense interest. It was perhaps strange that, extraordinary though it was, he never for one moment seemed to doubt the truth of what he heard. When Burton had finished, he rose to his feet in a state of great excitement.

"This is indeed wonderful," he declared. "It is more wonderful, even, than you can know of. The legend of the perfect food appears in the manuscripts of many centuries. It antedates literature by generations. There is a tomb in the interior of Japan, sacred to a saint who for seventy years worked for the production of this very bean. That, let me tell you, was three thousand years ago. My young friend, you have indeed been favored!"

"Let me understand this thing," Burton said, anxiously. "Those pages say that if one eats a green leaf after the bean, the change wrought in one will become absolutely permanent?"

"That is so," the professor assented. "Now all that you have to do, is to eat a green leaf from the little tree. After that, you will have no more need of those three beans, and you can therefore give them to me."

Burton made no attempt to produce his little silver box.

"First of all," he said, "I must test the truth of this. I cannot run any risks. I must go and eat a leaf. If in three months no change has taken place in me, I will lend you a bean to examine. I can do no more than that. Until this matter is absolutely settled, they are worth more than life itself to me."

Mr. Cowper seemed annoyed.

"Surely," he protested, "you are not going to ask me to wait three months until I can examine one of these?"

"Three months will soon pass," Burton replied. "Until that time is up, I could not part with them."

"But you can't imagine," the professor pleaded, "how marvelously interesting this is to me. Remember that I have spent all my life digging about among the archives and the literature and the superstitions of these pre-Egyptian peoples. You are the first man in the world, outside a little circle of fellow-workers, to speak to me of this perfect food. Your story as to how it came into your hands is the most amazing romance I have ever heard. It confirms many of my theories. It is wonderful. Do you realize what has happened? You, sir, you in your insignificant person," the professor continued, shaking his finger at his visitor, "have tasted the result of thousands of years of unceasing study. Wise men in their cells, before Athens was built, before the Pyramids were conceived, were thinking out this matter in strange parts of Egypt, in forgotten parts of Syria and Asia. For generations their dream has been looked upon as a thing elusive as the philosopher's stone, the transmutation of metals—any of these unsolved problems. For five hundred years—since the days of a Russian scientist who lived on the Black Sea, but whose name, for the moment, I have forgotten—the whole subject has lain dead. It is indeed true that the fairy tales of one generation become the science of the next. Our own learned men have been blind. The whole chain of reasoning is so clear. Every article of human food contains its separate particles, affecting the moral as well as the physical system. Why should it have been deemed necromancy to endeavor to combine these parts, to evolve by careful elimination and change the perfect food? In the house, young man, which you have told me of, there died the hero of the greatest discovery which has ever been made since the world began to spin upon its orbit."

"Will Miss Edith be back to-morrow?" Burton asked.

The professor stared at him.

"Miss Edith?" he repeated. "Oh! my daughter? Is she not in?"

"She is away for two days, your servant told me," Burton replied.

"Perhaps so—perhaps so," the professor agreed. "She has gone to her aunt's, very likely, in Chelsea. My sister has a house there in Bromsgrove Terrace."

Burton rose to his feet. He held out his hand for the manuscript.

"I am exceedingly obliged to you," he said. "Now I must go."

The professor gripped the manuscript in his hand. He was no longer a harmless and benevolent old gentleman. He was like a wild animal about to be robbed of its prey.

"No," he cried. "You must not take these away. You must not think of it. They are of no use to you. Leave me the sheets, just as they are. I will go further back. There are several words at the meaning of which I have only guessed. Leave them with me for a few days, and I will make you an exact translation."

"Very well," Burton assented.

"And one bean?" the professor begged. "Leave me one bean only? I promise not to eat it, not to dissect it, not to subject it to experiments of any sort. Let me just have it to look at, to be sure that what you have told me is not an hallucination."

Burton shook his head.

"I dare not part with one. I am going straight back to test the leaf theory. If it is correct, I will keep my promise. And—will you remember me to Miss Edith when she returns, professor?"

"To Miss Edith? Yes, yes, of course," Mr. Cowper declared, impatiently. "When shall you be down again, my young friend?" he went on earnestly. "I want to hear more of your experiences. I want you to tell me the whole thing over again. I should like to get a signed statement from you. There are several points in connection with what you say, which bear out a favorite theory of mine."

"I will come in a few days, if I may," Burton assured him.

The professor walked with his guest to the front door. He seemed reluctant to let him go.

"Take care of yourself, Mr. Burton," he enjoined. "Yours is a precious life. On no account subject yourself to any risks. Be careful of the crossings. Don't expose yourself to inclement weather. Keep away from any place likely to harbor infectious disease. I should very much like to have a meeting in London of a few of my friends, if I could ensure your presence."

"When I come down again," Burton promised, "we will discuss it."

He shook hands and hurried away. In less than an hour and a half he was in Mr. Waddington's rooms. The latter had just arrived from the office.

"Mr. Waddington," Burton exclaimed, "the little tree on which the beans grew—where is it?"

Mr. Waddington was taken aback.

"But I picked all the beans," he replied. "There were only the leaves left."

"Never mind that!" Burton cried. "It is the leaves we want! The tree— where is it? Quick! I want to feel myself absolutely safe."

Mr. Waddington's face was blank.

"You have heard the translation of those sheets?"

"I have," Burton answered hastily. "I will tell you all about it directly— as soon as you have brought me the tree."

Mr. Waddington had turned a little pale.

"I gave it to a child in the street, on my way home from Idlemay House," he declared. "There was no sign of any more beans coming and I had more than enough to carry."

Burton sank into a chair and groaned.

"We are lost," he exclaimed, "unless you can find that child! Our cure is only temporary. We need a leaf each from the tree. I have only eight months and two weeks more!"

Mr. Waddington staggered to a seat. He produced his own beans and counted them eagerly.

"A little under eleven months!" he muttered. "We must find the tree!"

XV

The Professor Insists

C rouched over his writing table, with sheets of manuscript on every side of him, Burton worked like a slave at his novel. After a week devoted by Mr. Waddington and himself to a fruitless search for the missing plant, they had handed the matter over to a private detective and Burton had settled down to make the most of the time before him. Day after day of strange joys had dawned and passed away. He had peopled his room with shadows. Edith had looked at him out of her wonderful eyes, he had felt the touch of her fingers as she had knelt by his side, the glow which had crept into his heart as he had read to her fragments of his story and listened to her words of praise. The wall which he had built stood firm and fast. He lived in his new days. Life was all foreground, and hour by hour the splendid fancies came.

It was his first great effort at composition. Those little studies of his, as he had passed backwards and forwards through the streets and crowded places, had counted for little. Here he was making serious demands upon his new capacity. In a sense it was all very easy, all very wonderful, yet sometimes dejection came. Then his head drooped upon his folded arms, he doubted himself and his work, he told himself that he was living in a fool's Paradise—a fool's Paradise indeed!

One afternoon there came a timid knock at his door. He turned in his chair a little impatiently. Then his pen slipped from his fingers. His left hand gripped the side of the table, his right hand the arm of his chair. It was a dream, of course!

"I hope we do not disturb you, Mr. Burton?" the professor inquired, with anxious amiability. "My daughter and I were in the neighborhood and I could not resist the visit. We had some trouble at first in finding you."

Burton rose to his feet. He was looking past the professor, straight into Edith's eyes. In her white muslin gown, her white hat and flowing white veil, she seemed to him more wonderful, indeed, than any of those cherished fancies of her which had passed through his room night and day to the music of his thoughts.

"I am glad," he said simply. "Of course I am glad to see you! Please come in. It is very untidy here. I have been hard at work."

He placed chairs for them. The professor glanced around the room with some satisfaction. It was bare, but there was nothing discordant upon the walls or in the furniture. There were many evidences, too, of a scholarly and cultivated taste. Edith had glided past him to the window and was murmuring her praises of the view.

"I have never seen a prettier view of the river in my life," she declared, "and I love your big window. It is almost like living out of doors, this. And how industrious you have been!"

She pointed to the sea of loose sheets which covered the table and the floor. He smiled. He was beginning to recover himself.

"I have been working very hard," he admitted.

"But why?" she murmured. "You are young. Surely there is plenty of time? Is it because the thoughts have come to you and you dared not daily with them? Or is it because you are like every one else—in such a terrible hurry to become rich and famous?"

He shook his head.

"It is not that," he said. "I have no thought of either. Alas!" he added, looking into her eyes, "I lack the great incentive!"

"Then why is it?" she whispered.

"You must not ask our young friend too many questions," the professor interrupted, a trifle impatiently. "Tell me, Mr. Burton, has there been any change—er—in your condition?"

Burton shivered for a moment.

"None at present," he admitted. "It is scarcely due as yet."

Mr. Cowper drew his chair a little nearer. His face betokened the liveliest interest. Edith stood in the window for a moment and then sank into a chair in the background.

"With reference to your last remark," the professor went on, "it has yet, I think, to be proved that these beans are of equal potency. You understand me, I am sure, Mr. Burton? I mean that it does not in the least follow that because one of them is able to keep you in an abnormal condition for two months, the next one will keep you there for the same period."

Burton was frankly startled.

"Is there anything about that in the translation, sir?" he asked.

"There is this sentence which I will read to you," the professor pronounced, drawing a roll of paper from his pocket and adjusting his spectacles. "I have now a more or less correct translation of the sheets you left with me, a copy of which is at your disposal. Here it is:—'*The formula is now enunciated and proved. The secret which has defied the sages of the world since the ages of twilight, has yielded itself to me, the nineteenth seeker after the truth in one direct line. One slight detail alone baffles me. So far as I have gone at present, the constituent parts, containing always the same elements and producing, therefore, the same effect, appear in variable dimensions or potencies, for reasons which at present elude me. Of my formula there is no longer any doubt. This substance which I have produced shall purify and make holy the world.'*"

The professor looked up from his paper.

"Our interesting friend," he remarked, "seems to have been interrupted at this point, probably by the commencement of that illness which had, unfortunately, a fatal conclusion. Yet the meaning of what he writes is perfectly clear. This substance, consolidated, I believe, into what you term a bean, is not equally distributed. Therefore, I take it that you may remain in your present condition for a longer or shorter period of time. The potency of the first—er—dose, is nothing to go by. You have, however, already learned how to render your present condition eternal."

Burton sighed.

"The knowledge came too late," he said. "The tree had disappeared. It was given away, by the Mr. Waddington I told you of, to a child whom he met in the street."

"Dear me!" Mr. Cowper exclaimed gravely. "This is most disappointing. Is there no chance of recovering it?"

"We are trying," Burton replied. "Mr. Waddington has engaged a private detective and we are also advertising in the papers."

"You have the beans still, at any rate," the professor remarked, hopefully.

"We have the beans," Burton admitted, "but it is very awkward not knowing how long one's condition is going to last. I might go out without my beans one day, and find myself assailed by all manner of amazing inclinations."

"My dear young man," the professor said earnestly, "let me point out to you that this is a wonderful position in which you have been placed. You ought to be most proud and grateful. Any trifling inconveniences which may result should be, I venture to say, utterly ignored by you. Now come, let me ask you a question. Are you feeling absolutely your—how shall I call it—revised self to-day?"

"Absolutely, thank Heaven!" Burton declared, fervently.

The professor nodded his head. All the time his eyes were roving about Burton's person, as though he were longing to make a minute study of his anatomy.

"It would be most interesting," he said, "to trace the commencement of any change in your condition. I am here with a proposition, Mr. Burton. I appeal to you in the name of science as well as—er—hospitality. The change might come to you here while you are alone. There would be no one to remark upon it, no one to make those interesting and instructive notes which, in justice to the cause of progress, should be made by some competent person such as—forgive me—myself. I ask you, therefore, to pack up and return with us to Leagate. You shall have a study to yourself, my daughter will be only too pleased and proud to assist you in your work, and I have also a young female who comes to type-write for me, whose services you can entirely command. I trust that you will not hesitate, Mr. Burton. We are most anxious—indeed we are most anxious, are we not, Edith?—to have you come."

Burton turned his head and glanced toward the girl. She had raised her veil. Her eyes met his, met his question and evaded it. She studied the pattern of the carpet. When she looked up again, her cheeks were pink.

"Mr. Burton will be very welcome," she said.

There was a short silence in the room. The sunshine fell across the dusty room in a long, quivering shaft. Outside, the branches of an elm tree swinging in the wind cast a shadow across the floor. The professor, with folded arms, sat alert and expectant. Burton, pale and shrunken with the labors of the last ten days, looked out of his burning eyes at the girl. For a single moment she had raised her head, had met his fierce inquiry with a certain wistful pathos, puzzling, an incomplete sentiment. Now she, too, was sitting as though in an attitude of waiting. Burton felt his heart suddenly leap. What might lie beyond the wall was of no account. He was a man with only a few brief months to live, as he had come to understand life. He would follow the eternal philosophy. He would do as the others and make the best of them.

"It is very kind of you," he said. "I am not prepared to make a visit,—I mean my clothes, and that sort of thing,—but if you will take me as I am, I will come with pleasure."

Mr. Cowper's face showed the liveliest satisfaction. Edith, on the other hand, never turned her head, although she felt Burton's eyes upon her.

"Capital!" the professor declared. "Now do not think that we are trying to abduct you, but there is a motor-car outside. We are going to take you straight home. You can have a little recreation this beautiful afternoon—a walk on the moors, or some tennis with Edith here. We will try and give you a pleasant time. You must collect your work now and go and put your things together. We are not in the least hurry. We will wait."

Burton rose a little unsteadily to his feet. He was weary with much labor, carried a little away by this wonderful prospect of living in the same house, of having her by his side continually. It was too amazing to realize. His heart gave a great leap as she moved towards him and looked a little shyly into his face.

"May I not help you to pick up these sheets? I see that you have numbered them all. I will keep them in their proper order. Perhaps you could trust me to do that while you went and packed your bag?"

"Quite right, my dear—quite right," the professor remarked, approvingly. "You will find my daughter most careful in such matters, Mr. Burton. She is used to being associated with work of importance."

"You are very kind," Burton murmured. "If you will excuse me, then, for a few moments?"

"By all means," the professor declared. "And pray suit yourself entirely, Mr. Burton, as to the clothes you bring and the preparations you make for your visit. If you prefer not to change for the evening, I will do the same. I am renowned in the neighborhood chiefly for my shabbiness and my carpet slippers."

Burton paused on the threshold and looked back. Edith was bending over the table, collecting the loose sheets of manuscript. The sunlight had turned her hair almost to the color of flame. Against the background of the open window, her slim, delicate figure, clad in a fashionable mist of lace and muslin, seemed to him like some wonderful piece of intensely modern statuary. Between them the professor sat, with his arms still folded, a benevolent yet pensive smile upon his lips.

XVI

Enter Mr. Bomford!

"I have decided," Edith remarked, stopping the swinging of the hammock with her foot, "to write and ask Mr. Bomford to come and spend the week-end here."

Burton shook his head.

"Please don't think of it," he begged. "It would completely upset me. I should not be able to do another stroke of work."

"You and your work!" Edith murmured, looking down at him. "What about me? What is the use of being engaged if I may not have my fiancé come and see me sometimes?"

"You don't want him," Burton declared, confidently.

"But I do," she insisted, "if only to stop your making love to me."

"I do not make love to you," he asserted. "I am in love with you. There is a difference."

"But you ought not to be in love with me—you have a wife," she reminded him.

"A wife who lives at Garden Green does not count," he assured her. "Besides, it was the other fellow who married her. She isn't really my wife at all. It would be most improper of me to pretend that she was."

"You are much too complicated a person to live in the same house with," she sighed. "I shall do as I said. I shall ask Mr. Bomford down for the week-end."

"Then I shall go back to London," he pronounced, firmly.

A shadow fell across the grass.

"What's that—what's that?" the professor demanded, anxiously.

They both looked up quickly. The professor had just put in one of his unexpected appearances. He had a habit of shuffling about in felt slippers which were altogether inaudible.

"Miss Edith was speaking of asking a visitor—a Mr. Bomford—down for the week-end," Burton explained suavely. "I somehow felt that I should not like him. In any case, I have been here for a week and I really ought—"

"Edith will do nothing of the sort," the professor declared, sharply.

"Do you hear that, Edith? No one is to be asked here at all. Mr. Burton's convenience is to be consulted before any one's."

She yawned and made a face at Burton.

"Very well, father," she replied meekly, "only I might just as well not be engaged at all."

"Just as well!" the professor snapped. "Such rubbish!"

Edith swung herself upright in the hammock, arranged her skirts, and faced her father indignantly.

"How horrid of you!" she exclaimed. "You know that I only got engaged to please you, because you thought that Mr. Bomford would take more interest in publishing your books. If I can't ever have him here, I shall break it off. He expects to be asked—I am quite sure he does."

The professor frowned impatiently.

"You are a most unreasonable child," he declared. "Mr. Bomford may probably pay us a passing visit at any time, and you must be content with that."

Edith sighed. She contemplated the tips of her shoes for some moments.

"I do seem to be in trouble to-day," she remarked,—"first with Mr. Burton and then with you."

The professor turned unsympathetically away.

"You know perfectly well how to keep out of it," he said, making his way toward the house.

"Between you both," Edith continued, "I really am having rather a hard time. This is the last straw of all. I am deprived of my young man now, just to please you."

"He isn't a young man," Burton contradicted.

Edith clasped her hands behind her head and looked fixedly up at the blue sky.

"Never mind his age," she murmured. "He is really very nice."

"I've seen his photograph in the drawing-room," Burton reminded her.

Edith frowned.

"He is really much better looking than that," she said with emphasis.

"It is perhaps as well," Burton retorted, "especially if he is in the habit of going about unattended."

Edith ignored his last speech altogether. "Mr. Bomford is also," she went on, "extremely pleasant and remarkably well-read. His manners are charming."

"I am sorry you are missing him so much," Burton said.

"A girl," Edith declared, with her head in the air, "naturally misses the small attentions to which she is accustomed from her fiancé."

"If there is anything an unworthy substitute can do," Burton began,—

"Nice girls do not accept substitutes for their fiancés," Edith interrupted, ruthlessly. "I am a very nice girl indeed. I think that you are very lazy this afternoon. You would be better employed at work than in talking nonsense."

Burton sighed.

"I tried to work this morning," he declared. "I gave up simply because I found myself thinking of you all the time. Genius is so susceptible to diversions. This afternoon I couldn't settle down because I was wondering all the time whether you were wearing blue linen or white muslin. I just looked out of the window to see—you were asleep in the hammock. . . you witch!" he murmured softly. "How could I keep sane and collected! How could I write about anybody or anything in the world except you! The wind was blowing those little strands of hair over your face. Your left arm was hanging down—so; why is an arm such a graceful thing, I wonder? Your left knee was drawn up—you had been supporting a book against it and—"

"I don't want to hear another word," Edith protested quickly.

He sighed.

"It took me about thirty seconds to get down," he murmured. "You hadn't moved."

"Shall we have tea out here or in the study?" Edith asked.

"Anywhere so long as we escape from this," Burton replied, gazing across the lawn. "What is it?"

A man was making his way from the house towards them, a man who certainly presented a somewhat singular appearance. He was wearing a long linen duster, a motor-cap which came over his ears, and a pair of goggles which he was busy removing. Edith swung herself on to her feet. Considering her late laments, the dismay in her tone was a little astonishing.

"It is Mr. Bomford!" she cried.

Burton sighed—with relief.

"I am glad to hear that it is human," he murmured. "I thought that it was a Wells nightmare or that something from underground had been let loose."

She shot an indignant glance at him. Her greeting of Mr. Bomford was almost enough to turn his head. She held out both her hands.

"My dear Mr.—my dear Paul!" she exclaimed. "How glad I am to see you! Have you motored down?"

"Obviously, my dear, obviously," the newcomer remarked, removing further portions of his disguise and revealing a middle-aged man of medium height and unimposing appearance, with slight sandy whiskers and moustache. "A very hot and dusty ride too. Still, after your father's message I did not hesitate for a second. Where is he, Edith? Have you any idea what it is that he wants?"

She shook her head.

"Did he send for you?" she asked.

"Send for me!" Mr. Bomford repeated. "I should rather think he did."

He looked inquiringly towards Burton. Edith introduced them.

"This," she said, "is Mr. Burton, a friend of father's, who is staying with us for a few days. He is writing a book. Perhaps, if you are very polite to him, he will let you publish it. Mr. Bomford—Mr. Burton."

The two men shook hands solemnly. Neither of them expressed any pleasure at the meeting.

"I am sure you would like a drink," Edith suggested. "Let me take you up to the house and we can find father. You won't mind, Mr. Burton?"

"Not in the least," he assured her.

They disappeared into the house. Burton threw himself once more upon the lawn, his hands clasped behind his head, gazing upwards through the leafy boughs to the blue sky. So this was Mr. Bomford! This was the rival of whom he had heard! Not so very formidable a person, not formidable at all save for one thing only—he was free to marry her, free to marry Edith. Burton lay and dreamed in the sunshine. A thrush came out and sang to him. A west wind brought him wafts of perfume from the gardens below. The serenity of the perfect afternoon mocked his disturbed frame of mind. What was the use of it all? The longer he remained here the more abject he became! . . . Suddenly Edith reappeared alone. She came across the lawn to him with a slight frown upon her forehead. He lay there and watched her until the last moment. Then he rose and dragged out a chair for her.

"So the lovers' interview is over!" he ventured to observe. "You do not seem altogether transported with delight."

"I am very much pleased indeed to see Mr. Bomford," she assured him.

"I," he murmured, "am glad that I have seen him."

Edith looked at him covertly.

"I do not think," she said, "that I quite approve of your tone this afternoon."

"I am quite sure," he retorted, "that I do not approve of yours."

She made a little grimace at him.

"Let us agree, then, to be mutually dissatisfied. I do wish," she added softly, "that I knew why father had sent for Mr. Bomford. It is nothing to do with his work, I am sure of that. He knows that Paul hates coming away from the office on week days."

Burton groaned.

"Is his name Paul?"

"Certainly it is," she answered.

"It sounds very familiar."

"It is nothing of the sort; when you are engaged to a person, you naturally call him by his Christian name. I can't think, though, why father didn't tell us that he was coming."

"I have an idea," Burton declared, "that his coming has something to do with me."

"With you?

"Why not? Am I not an interesting subject for speculation? Mr. Bomford, you told me only a few days ago, is a scientist, an Egyptologist, a philosopher. Why should he not be interested in the same things which interest your father?"

"It is quite true," she admitted. "I had not thought of that."

"At the present moment," Burton continued, moving a little on one side, "they are probably in the dining-room drinking Hock and seltzer, and your father is explaining to your fiancé the phenomenon of my experiences. I wonder whether he will believe them?"

"Mr. Bomford," she said, "will believe anything that my father tells him."

"Are you very much in love?" Burton asked, irrelevantly.

"You ask such absurd questions," she replied. "Nowadays, one is never in love."

"How little you know of what goes on nowadays!" he sighed. "What about myself? Do I need to tell you that I am hopelessly in love with you?"

"You," she declared, "are a phenomenon. You do not count."

The professor and his guest came through the French window, arm in arm, talking earnestly.

"Look at them!" Burton groaned. "They are talking about me—I can tell it by their furtive manner. Mr. Bomford has heard the whole story. He is a little incredulous but he wishes to be polite to his future father-in-law. What a pity that I could not have a relapse while he is here!"

"Couldn't you?" she exclaimed. "It would be such fun!"

Burton shook his head.

"Nothing but the truth," he declared sadly.

Mr. Bomford, without his motoring outfit, was still an unprepossessing figure. He wore a pince-nez; his manner was fussy and inclined to be a little patronizing. He had the air of an unsuccessful pedagogue. He was obviously regarding Burton with a new interest. During tea-time he conversed chiefly with Edith, who seemed a little nervous, and answered most of his questions with monosyllables. Burton and the professor were silent. Burton was watching Edith and the professor was watching Burton. As soon as the meal was concluded, the professor rose to his feet.

"Edith, my dear," he said, "we wish you to leave us for a minute or two. Mr. Bomford and I have something to say to Mr. Burton."

Edith, with a slight shrug of the shoulders, rose to her feet. She caught a glance from Burton and turned at once to her fiancé.

"Am I to be taken for a ride this evening?" she asked.

"A little later on, by all means, my dear Edith," Mr. Bomford declared. "A little later on, certainly. Your father has kindly invited me to stay and dine. It will give me very much pleasure. Perhaps we could go for a short distance in—say three-quarters of an hour's time?"

Edith went slowly back to the house. Burton watched her disappear. The professor and Mr. Bomford drew their chairs a little closer. The professor cleared his throat.

"Mr. Burton," he began, "Mr. Bomford and I have a proposition to lay before you. May I beg for your undivided attention?"

Burton withdrew his eyes from the French window through which Edith had vanished.

"I am quite at your service," he answered quietly. "Please let me hear exactly what it is that you have to say."

XVII

Burton Declines

The professor cleared his throat.

"In the first place, Mr. Burton," he said, "I feel that I owe you an apology. I have taken a great liberty. Mr. Bomford here is one of my oldest and most intimate friends. I have spoken to him of the manuscript you brought me to translate. I have told him your story."

Mr. Bomford scratched his side whiskers and nodded patronizingly.

"It is a very remarkable story," he declared, "a very remarkable story indeed. I can assure you, Mr.—Mr. Burton, that I never listened to anything so amazing. If any one else except my old friend here had told me of it, I should have laughed. I should have dismissed the whole thing at once as incredible and preposterous. Even now, I must admit that I find it almost impossible to accept the story in its entirety."

Burton looked him coldly in the eyes. Mr. Bomford did not please him.

"The story is perfectly true," he said. "There is not the slightest necessity for you to believe it—in fact, so far as I am concerned, it does not matter in the least whether you do or not."

"Mr. Burton," the professor interposed, "I beg that you will not misunderstand Mr. Bomford. His is not a militant disbelief, it is simply a case of suspended judgment. In the meantime, assuming the truth of what you have told us—and I for one, you must remember, Mr. Burton, have every faith in your story—assuming its truth, Mr. Bomford has made a most interesting proposition."

Burton, with half-closed eyes, was listening to the singing of a thrush and watching the sunshine creep through the dark foliage of the cedar trees. He was only slightly interested.

"A proposition?" he murmured.

"Precisely," Mr. Cowper assented. "We have an appeal to make to you, an appeal on behalf of science, an appeal on behalf of your fellow-creatures, an appeal on behalf of yourself. Your amazing experience is one which should be analyzed and given to the world."

"What you want, I suppose," Burton remarked, "is one of my beans."

"Exactly," the professor admitted, eagerly.

"I have already," Burton said, "done my best to make you understand my feelings in this matter. Those beans represent everything to me. Nothing would induce me to part with a single one."

"We can understand that," the professor agreed. "We are approaching you with regard to them in an altogether different manner. Mr. Bomford is a man of business. It is our wish to make you an offer."

"You mean that you would like to buy one?"

"Precisely," the professor replied. "We are prepared to give you, between us, a thousand pounds for one of those beans."

Burton shook his head. The conversation appeared to be totally devoid of interest to him.

"A thousand pounds," he said, "is, I suppose, a great deal of money. I have never owned so much in my life. But money, after all, is only valuable for what it can buy. Each one of my beans means two months, perhaps more, of real life. No money could buy that."

"My young friend," the professor insisted solemnly, "you are looking at this matter from a selfish point of view. Experiences such as you have passed through, belong to the world. You are merely the agent, the fortunate medium, through which they have materialized."

Burton shrugged his shoulders.

"So far," he replied, "I owe no debt to humanity. The longer I live and the wiser I get, the more I realize the absolute importance of self-care. Individualism is the only real and logical creed. No one else looks after your interests. No one else in the world save yourself is of any real account."

"A thousand pounds," Mr. Bomford interposed, "is a great deal of money for a young man in your position."

"It is a very great deal," Burton admitted. "But what you and Mr. Cowper both seem to forget is the very small part that money plays in the acquisition of real happiness. Money will not buy the joy which makes life worth living, it will not buy the power to appreciate, the power to discriminate. It will not buy taste or the finer feelings, without the possession of which one becomes a dolt, a thing that creeps about the face of the world. I thank you for your offer, professor, and Mr. Bomford, but I have nothing to sell. If you would excuse me!"

He half rose from his chair but Mr. Cowper thrust him back again.

"We have not finished yet, my dear Mr. Burton," he said eagerly. "You are making up your mind too hastily."

"A thousand pounds," Mr. Bomford repeated, condescendingly, "is a very useful sum. Those peculiar gifts of yours may vanish. Take the advice of a business man. Remember that you will still have two or three beans left. It is only one we ask for. I want to put the matter on as broad a basis as possible. We make our appeal on behalf of the cause of science. You must not refuse us." Burton rose to his feet determinedly. "Not only do I refuse," he said, "but it is not a matter which I am inclined to discuss any longer. I am sorry if you are disappointed, but my story was really told to Mr. Cowper here in confidence." He left them both sitting there. He found Edith in a corner of the long drawing-room. She was pretending to read.

"Whatever is the matter?" she asked. "I did not expect you so soon. I thought that Mr. Bomford and father wanted to talk to you." "So they did," he replied. "They made me a foolish offer. It was Mr. Bomford's idea, I am sure, not your father's. I am tired, Edith. Come and walk with me."—She glanced out of the window.

"I think," she said demurely, "that I am expected to go for a ride with Mr. Bomford."

"Then please disappoint him," he pleaded. "I do not like your friend Mr. Bomford. He is an egotistical and ignorant person. We will go across the moors, we will climb our little hill. Perhaps we might even wait there until the sunset."

"I am quite sure," she said decidedly, "that Mr. Bomford would not like that."

"What does it matter?" he answered. "A man like Mr. Bomford has no right to have any authority over you at all. You are of a different clay. I am sure that you will never marry him. If you will not walk with me, I shall work, and I am not in the humor for work. I shall probably spoil one of my best chapters."

She rose to her feet.

"In the interests of your novel!" she murmured. "Come! Only we had better go out by the back door."

Like children they stole out of the house. They climbed the rolling moorland till they reached the hill on the further side of the valley. She sat down, breathless, with her back against the trunk of a small Scotch fir. Burton threw himself on to the ground by her side.

"We think too much always of consequences," he said "After this evening, what does anything matter? The gorse is a flaming yellow; do you see how it looks like a field of gold there in the distance? Only the haze separates it from the blue sky. Look down where I am pointing, Edith. It was there by the side of the road that I first looked into the garden and saw you."

"It was not you who looked," she objected, shaking her head. "It was the other man."

"What part is it that survives?" he asked, a little bitterly. "Why should the new man be cursed with memory? Don't you think that even then there must have been two of me, one struggling against the other—one seeking for the big things, one laying hold of the lower? We are all like that, Edith! Even now I sometimes feel the tug, although it leads in other directions."

"To Garden Green?" she murmured.

"Never that," he answered fiercely, "and you know it. There are lower heights, though, in the most cultured of lives. There are moments of madness, moments that carry one off one's feet, which come alike to the slave and his master. Dear Edith, up here one can talk. It is such a beautiful world. One can open one's eyes, one can breathe, one can look around him. It is the joy of simple things, the real true joy of life which beats in our veins. Do you think that we were made for unhappiness in such a world, Edith?"

"No!" she whispered, faintly.

"There isn't anything so beautiful to me upon God's earth," he continued, "as the love in my heart for you. I wanted to tell you so this evening. I have brought you here to tell you so—to this particular spot. Something tells me that it may be almost our last chance. I left those two whispering upon the lawn. What is it they are planning, I wonder? That man Bomford is no companion for your father. He has given him an idea about me and my story. What is it, I wonder? To rob me, to throw me out, to take my treasure from me by force?"

"You are my father's guest," she reminded him softly. "He will not forget it."

"There are greater things in the world," he went on, "than the obligations of hospitality. There are tides which sweep away the landmarks of nature herself. Your father is thirsty for knowledge. This man Bomford is his friend. There have been more crimes committed in the world for lofty motives than one hears of."

He leaned a little forward. They could see the smoke curling up from the house below, its gardens laid out like patchwork, the low house itself covered with creepers.

"It was an idyll, that," he went on. "Bomford's trail is about the place now, the trail of some poisonous creature. Nothing will ever be the same. I want to remember this last evening. I have looked upon life from the hill tops and I have looked at it along the level ways, but I have seen nothing in it so beautiful, I have felt nothing in it so wonderful, as my love for you. You were a dream to me before, half hidden, only partly realized. Soon you will be a dream to me again. But never, never, dear, since the magic brush painted the blue into the skies, the purple on to the heather, the green on to the grass, the yellow into the gorse, the blue into your eyes, was there any love like mine!"

She leaned towards him. Her fingers were cold and her voice trembled.

"You must not!" she begged.

He smiled as he passed his arm around her.

"Are we not on the hill top, dear?" he said. "You need have no fear. Only to-night I felt that I must say these things to you, even though the passion which they represent remains as ineffective forever as the words themselves. I have a feeling, you know, that after to-day things will be different."

"Why should they be?" she asked. "In any case, your time cannot come yet."

Once more he looked downward into the valley. Like a little speck along the road a motor-car was crawling along.

"It is Mr. Bomford," he said. "He is coming to look for you."

She rose to her feet. Together they stood, for a moment, hand in hand, looking down upon the flaming landscape. The fields at their feet were brilliant with color; in the far distance the haze of the sea. Their fingers were locked.

"Mr. Bomford," he sighed, "is coming up the hill."

"Then I think," she said quietly, "that we had better go down!"

XVIII

THE END OF A DREAM

Dinner that evening was a curious meal, partly constrained, partly enlivened by strange little bursts of attempted geniality on the part of the professor. Mr. Bomford told long and pointless stories with much effort and the air of a man who would have made himself agreeable if he could. Edith leaned back in her chair, eating very little, her eyes large, her cheeks pale. She made her escape as soon as possible and Burton watched her with longing eyes as he passed out into the cool darkness. He half rose, indeed, to follow her, but his host and Mr. Bomford both moved their chairs so that they sat on either side of him. The professor filled the glasses with his own hand. It was his special claret, a wonderful wine, the cobwebbed bottle of which, reposing in a wicker cradle, he handled with jealous care.

"Mr. Burton," he began, settling down in his chair, "we have been unjust to you, Mr. Bomford and I. We apologize. We ask your forgiveness."

"Unjust?" Burton murmured.

"Unjust," the professor repeated. "I allude to this with a certain amount of shame. We made you an offer of a thousand pounds for a portion of that—er—peculiar product to which you owe this wonderful change in your disposition. We were in the wrong. We had thoughts in our mind which we should have shared with you. It was not fair, Mr. Burton, to attempt to carry out such a scheme as Mr. Bomford here had conceived, without including you in it." The professor nodded to himself, amiably satisfied with his words. Burton remained mystified. Mr. Bomford took up the ball.

"We yielded, Mr. Burton," he said, "to the natural impulse of all business men. We tried to make the best bargain we could for ourselves. A little reflection and—er—your refusal of our offer, has brought us into what I trust you will find a more reasonable frame of mind. We wish now to treat you with the utmost confidence. We wish to lay our whole scheme before you."

"I don't know what you mean," Burton declared, a little wearily. "You want one of my beans, for which you offered a certain sum of money.

I am sorry. I would give you one if I could, but I cannot spare it. They are all that stand between me and a relapse into a state of being which I shudder to contemplate. Need we discuss it any further? I think, if you do not mind—"

He half rose to his feet, his eyes were searching the shadows of the garden. The professor pulled him down.

"Be reasonable, Mr. Burton—be reasonable," he begged. "Listen to what Mr. Bomford has to say."

Mr. Bomford cleared his throat, scratched his chin for a moment thoughtfully, and half emptied his glass of claret.

"Our scheme, my young friend," He said condescendingly, "is worthy even of your consideration. You are, I understand, gifted with some powers of observation which you have turned to lucrative account. It has naturally occurred to you, then, in your studies of life, that the greatest accumulations of wealth which have taken place during the present generation have come entirely through discoveries, which either nominally or actually have affected the personal well-being of the individual. Do I make myself clear?

"I have no doubt," Burton murmured, "that I shall understand presently."

"Once convince a man," Mr. Bomford continued, "that you are offering him something which will improve his health, and he is yours, or rather his money is—his two and sixpence or whatever particular sum you may have designed to relieve him of. It is for that reason that you see the pages of the magazines and newspapers filled with advertisements of new cures for ancient diseases. There is more money in the country than there has ever been, but there are just the same number of real and fancied diseases. Mankind is, if possible, more credulous to-day than at any epoch during our history. There are millions who will snatch at the slightest chance of getting rid of some real or fancied ailment. Great journals have endeavored to persuade us that you can attain perfect health by standing on your head in the bathroom for ten minutes before breakfast. A million bodies, distorted into strange shapes, can be seen every morning in the domestic bed-chamber. A health-food made from old bones has been one of the brilliant successes of this generation. Now listen to my motto. This is what I want to bring home to every inhabitant of this country. This is what I want to see in great black type in every newspaper, on every hoarding, and if possible flashed at night upon the sky: 'Cure the mind first; the mind will cure the body.'

That," Mr. Bomford concluded, modestly, "is my idea of one of our preliminary advertisements."

The professor nodded approvingly. Burton glanced from one to the other of the two men with an air of almost pitiful non-comprehension. Mr. Bomford, having emptied his glass of claret, started afresh.

"My idea, in short," he went on, "is this. Let us three join forces. Let us analyze this marvelous product, into the possession of which you, Mr. Burton, have so mysteriously come. Let us, blending its constituents as nearly as possible, place upon the market a health-food not for the body but for the mind. You follow me now, I am sure? Menti-culture is the craze of the moment. It would become the craze of the million but for a certain vagueness in its principles, a certain lack of appeal to direct energies. We will preach the cause. We will give the public something to buy. We will ask them ten and sixpence a time and they will pay it gladly. What is more, Mr. Burton, the public will pay it all over the world. America will become our greatest market. Nothing like this has ever before been conceived, 'Leave your bodies alone for a time,' we shall say. 'Take our food and improve your moral system.' We shall become the crusaders of commerce. Your story will be told in every quarter of the globe, it will be translated into every conceivable tongue. Your picture will very likely adorn the lid of our boxes. It will be a matter for consideration, indeed, whether we shall not name this great discovery after you."

"So it was for this," Burton exclaimed, "that you offered me that thousand pounds!"

"We were to blame," Mr. Bomford admitted.

"Very much to blame," the professor echoed.

"Nevertheless," Mr. Bomford insisted, "it is an incident which you must forget. It is man's first impulse, is it not, to make the best bargain he can for himself? We tried it and failed. For the future we abandon all ideas of that sort, Mr. Burton. We associate you, both nominally and in effect, with our enterprise, in which we will be equal partners. The professor will find the capital, I will find the commercial experience, you shall hand over the bean. I promise you that before five years have gone by, you shall be possessed of wealth beyond any dreams you may ever have conceived."

Burton moved uneasily in his chair.

"But I have never conceived any dreams of wealth at all," he objected. "I have no desire whatever to be rich. Wealth seems to me to be only an additional excitement to vulgarity. Besides, the possession of wealth in itself tends to an unnatural state of existence. Man is happy only if he earns the money which buys for him the necessaries of life."

Mr. Bomford listened as one listens to a lunatic. Mr. Cowper, however, nodded his head in kindly toleration.

"Thoughts like that," he admitted, "have come to me, my young friend, in the seclusion of my study. They have come, perhaps, in the inspired moments, but in the inspired moments one is not living that every-day and necessary life which is forced upon us by the conditions of existence in this planet. There is nothing in the whole scheme of life so great as money. With it you can buy the means of gratifying every one of those unnatural desires with which Fate has endowed us. Take my case, for instance. If this wealth comes to me, I shall spend no more upon what I eat or drink or wear, yet, on the other hand, I shall gratify one of the dreams of my life. I shall start for the East with a search party, equipped with every modern invention which the mind of man has conceived. I shall go from site to site of the ruined cities of Egypt. No one can imagine what treasures I may not discover. I shall even go on to a part of Africa—but I need not weary you with this. I simply wanted you to understand that the desire for wealth is not necessarily vulgar."

Burton yawned slightly. His eyes sought once more the velvety shadows which hung over the lawn. He wondered down which of those dim avenues she had passed.

"I am so sorry," he said apologetically. "You are a man of business, Mr. Bomford, and you, professor, see much further into life than I can, but I do not wish to have anything whatever to do with your scheme. It does not appeal to me in the least—in fact it offends me. It seems crassly vulgar, a vulgar way of attaining to a position which I, personally, should loathe."

He rose to his feet.

"If you will excuse me, professor," he said. Mr. Bomford, with a greater show of vigor than he had previously displayed, jumped up and laid his hand upon the young man's shoulder. His hard face seemed suddenly to have become the rioting place for evil passions. His lips were a little parted and his teeth showed unpleasantly.

"Do you mean, young man," he exclaimed, "that you refuse to join us?"

"That is what I intended to convey," Burton replied coldly.

"You refuse either to come into our scheme or to give us one of the beans?"

Burton nodded.

"I hold them in trust for myself." There was a moment's silence. Mr. Bomford seemed to be struggling for words. The professor was looking exceedingly disappointed.

"Mr. Burton," he protested, "I cannot help feeling a certain amount of admiration for your point of view, but, believe me, you are entirely in the wrong. I beg that you will think this matter over."

"I am sure that it would be useless," Burton replied. "Nothing would induce me to change my mind."

"Nothing?" Mr. Bomford asked, with a peculiar meaning in his tone.

"Nothing?" the professor echoed softly.

Burton withdrew his eyes from the little shadowy vista of garden and looked steadfastly at the two men. Then his heart began to beat. He was filled with a sort of terror lest they should say what he felt sure was in their minds. It was like sacrilege. It was something unholy. His eyes had been caught by the flutter of a white gown passing across one of the lighter places of the perfumed darkness. They had been watching him. He only prayed that they would not interrupt until he had reached the end of his speech.

"Professor," he said softly, turning to his host, "there is one thing which I desire so greatly that I would give my life itself for it. I would give even what you have asked for to-night and be content to leave the world in so much shorter time. But that one thing I may not ask of you, for in those days of which I have told you, before the wonderful adventure came, I was married. My wife lives now in Garden Green. I have also a little boy. You will forgive me."

He passed through the open French windows and neither of them made any further attempt to detain him. Their silence was a little unnatural and from the walk outside he glanced for a moment behind him. The two men were sitting in exactly the same positions, their faces were turned towards him, and their eyes seemed to be following his movements. Yet there was a change. The professor was no longer the absorbed, mildly benevolent man of science. Mr. Bomford had lost his commonplace expression. There was a new thing in their faces, something eager, ominous. Burton felt a sudden depression as he turned away. He looked with relief at the thin circle of the moon, visible now through the waving elm trees at the bottom of the garden. He drew in with joy a long breath of the delicious perfume drawn by the night from the silent boughs of the cedar tree. Resolutely he hurried away from the sight of that ugly little framed picture upon which he had gazed through the open French windows—the two men on either side of the lamp, watching him.

"Edith!" he called softly.

She answered him with a little laugh. She was almost by his side. He took a quick step forward. She was standing among the deepest shadows, against the trunk of the cedar tree, her slim body leaning slightly against it. It seemed to him that her face was whiter, her eyes softer than ever. He took her hand in his.

She smiled.

"You must not come out to me here," she whispered. "Mr. Bomford will not like it. It is most improper."

"But it may be our good-bye," he pleaded. "They want me to do something, Mr. Bomford and your father, something hideous, utterly grotesque. I have refused and they are very angry."

"What is it that they want you to do?"

"Dear," he answered, "you, I am sure, will understand. They want me to give them one of my beans. They want to make some wretched drug or medicine from it, to advertise it all over the world, to amass a great fortune."

"Are you in earnest?" she cried.

"Absolutely," he assured her. "It is Mr. Bomford's scheme. He says that it would mean great wealth for all of us. Your father, too, praises it. He, too, seemed to come—for the moment, at any rate—under the curse. He, too, is greedy for money."

"And you?" she whispered. "What did you say?

"What did I say?" he repeated wonderingly. "But of course you know! Imagine the horror of it—a health-food for the mind! Huge sums of money rolling in from the pockets of credulous people, money stinking with the curse of vulgarity and quackery! It is almost like a false note, dear, to speak of it out here, but I must tell you because they are angry with me. I am afraid that your father will send me away, and I am afraid that our little dream is over and that I shall not wander with you any more evenings here in the cool darkness, when the heat of the day is past and the fragrance of the cedar tree and your roses fills the air, and you, your sweet self, Edith, are here."

She was looking at him very fixedly. Her lips were a little parted, her eyes were moist, her bosom was rising and falling as though she were shaken by some wonderful emotion.

"Dear!" she murmured.

It seemed to him that she leaned a little towards him. His heart ached with longing. Very slowly, almost reverently, his hands touched her shoulders, drew her towards him.

"You and I," he whispered, "at least we live in the same world. Nothing will ever be able to take the joy of that thought from my heart."

She remained quite passive. In her eyes there was a far-away look.

"Dear," she said softly in his ear, "you are such a dreamer, aren't you— such a dear unpractical person? Have you never used your wonderful imagination to ask yourself what money may really mean? You can buy a world of beautiful things, you can buy the souls of men and women, you can buy the law."

He felt a cold pain in his heart. Looking at her through the twilight he could almost fancy that there was a gleam in her face of something which he had seen shining out of her father's eyes. His arms fell away from her. The passion which had thrilled him but a moment ago seemed crushed by that great resurgent impulse which he was powerless to control.

"You think that I should do this?" he cried, hoarsely.

"Why not?" she answered. "Money is only vulgar if you spend it vulgarly. It might mean so much to you and to me."

"Tell me how?" he faltered.

"Mr. Bomford is very fond of money," she continued. "He is fonder of money, I think, than he is of me. And then," she added, her voice sinking to a whisper, "there is Garden Green. Of course, I do not know much about these things, but I suppose if you really wanted to, and spent a great deal of money, you could buy your freedom, couldn't you?"

The air seemed full of jangling discords. He closed his eyes. It was as though a shipwreck was going on around him. His dream was being broken up into pieces. The girl with the fair hair was passing into the shadows from which she had come. She called to him across the lawn as he hurried away, softly at first and then insistently. But Burton did not return. He spent his night upon the Common.

XIX

A Bad Half-Hour

Burton slept that night under a gorse bush. He was no sooner alone on the great unlit Common with its vast sense of spaciousness, its cool silence, its splendid dome of starlit sky, than all his anger and disappointment seemed to pass away. The white, threatening faces of the professor and Mr. Bomford no longer haunted him. Even the memory of Edith herself tugged no longer at his heartstrings. He slept almost like a child, and awoke to look out upon a million points of sunlight sparkling in the dewdrops. A delicious west wind was blowing. Little piled-up masses of white cloud had been scattered across the blue sky. Even the gorse bushes creaked and quivered. The fir trees in a little spinney close at hand were twisted into all manners of shapes. Burton listened to their music for a few minutes, and exchanged civilities with a dapple-breasted thrush seated on a clump of heather a few yards away. Then he rose to his feet, took in a long breath of the fresh morning air, and started briskly across the Common towards the nearest railway station.

He was conscious, after the first few steps, of a dim premonition of some coming change. It did not affect—indeed, it seemed to increase the lightness of his spirits, yet he was conscious at the back of his brain of a fear which he could not put into words. The first indication of real trouble came in the fact that he found himself whistling "Yip-i-addy-i-ay" as he turned into the station yard. He knew then what was coming.

After the first start, the rapidity of his collapse was appalling. The seclusion of the first-class carriage to which his ticket entitled him, and which his somewhat peculiar toilet certainly rendered advisable, was suddenly immensely distasteful. He bought Tit-bits and Ally Sloper at the bookstall, squeezed his way into a crowded third-class compartment, and joined in a noisy game of nap with half a dozen roistering young clerks, who were full of jokes about his crumpled dinner clothes. Arrived in London, he had the utmost difficulty to refrain from buying a red and yellow tie displayed in the station lavatory where he washed and shaved, and the necessity for purchasing a collar stud left him for a few moments in imminent peril of acquiring a large brass-stemmed production with a sham diamond head. He hastened to his rooms, scarcely daring to look about him, turned over the clothes in his wardrobe with a curious dissatisfaction, and dressed himself hastily in as offensive a combination of garments as he could lay his hands upon. He bought some common Virginian cigarettes and made his way to the offices of Messrs. Waddington and Forbes.

Mr. Waddington was unfeignedly glad to see him. His office was pervaded by a sort of studious calm which, from a business point of view, seemed scarcely satisfactory. Mr. Waddington himself appeared to be immersed in a calf-bound volume of Ruskin. He glanced curiously at his late employee.

"Did you dress in a hurry, Burton?" he inquired. "That combination of gray trousers and brown coat with a blue tie seems scarcely in your usual form."

Burton dragged up a chair to the side of his late employer's desk.

"Mr. Waddington," he begged, "don't let me go out of your sight until I have taken another bean. It came on early this morning. I went through all my wardrobe to find the wrong sort of clothes, and the only thing that seemed to satisfy me was to wear odd ones. Whatever you do, don't lose sight of me. In a few hours' time I shouldn't want to take a bean at all. I should be inviting you to lunch at the Golden Lion, playing billiards in the afternoon, and having a night out at a music hall."

Mr. Waddington nodded sympathetically.

"Poor fellow!" he said. "Seems odd that you should turn up this morning. I can sympathize with you. Have you noticed my tie?"

Burton nodded approvingly.

"Very pretty indeed," he declared.

"You won't think so when you've had that bean," Mr. Waddington groaned. "It began to come on with me about an hour ago. I forced myself into these clothes but the tic floored me. I've a volume of Ruskin here before me, but underneath, you see," he continued, lifting up the blotting-paper, "is a copy of Snapshots. I'm fighting it off as long as I can. The fact is I've a sale this afternoon. I thought if I could last until after that it might not be a bad thing."

"How's the biz?" Burton asked with a touch of his old jauntiness. "Going strong, eh?"

"Not so good and not so bad," Mr. Waddington admitted. "We've got over that boom that started at first when people didn't understand things. They seem to regard me now with a mixture of suspicion and contempt. All the same, we get a good many outside buyers in, and we've pulled along all right up till now. It's been the best few months of my life," Mr. Waddington continued, "by a long way, but I'm getting scared, and that's a fact."

"How many beans have you left?" Burton inquired.

"Four," Mr. Waddington replied. "What I shall do when they've gone I can't imagine."

Burton held his head for a moment a little wearily.

"There are times," he confessed, "especially when one's sort of between the two things like this, when I can't see my way ahead at all. Do you know that last night the man with whom I have been staying—a man of education too, who has been a professor at Oxford University,—and another, a more commercial sort of Johnny, offered me a third partnership in a great enterprise for putting on the market a new mental health-food, if I would give them one of the beans for analysis. They were convinced that we should make millions."

Mr. Waddington was evidently struck with the idea.

"It's a great scheme," he said hesitatingly. "I suppose last night it occurred to you that it was just a trifle—eh?—just a trifle vulgar?" he asked tentatively.

Burton assented gloomily.

"Last night," he declared, "it seemed to me like a crime. It made me shiver all over while they talked of it. To-day, well, I'm half glad and I'm half sorry that they're not here. If they walked into this office now I'd swallow a bean as quickly as I could, but I tell you frankly, Mr. Waddington, that at the present moment it seems entirely reasonable to me. Money, after all, is worth having, isn't it?—a nice comfortable sum so that one could sit back and just have a good time. Don't stare at me like that. Of course, I'm half ashamed of what I'm saying. There's the other part pulling and tugging away all the time makes me feel inclined to kick myself, but I can't help it. I know that these half formed ideas of enjoyment by means of wealth are only degrading, that one would sink—oh, hang it all, Mr. Waddington, what a mess it all is!"

Mr. Waddington pulled down his desk.

"We must go through with it, Burton," he said firmly. "You're more advanced than I am in this thing, I can see. You'll need your bean quickly. I believe I can hold off till after the sale. But—I've a curious sort of temptation at the present moment, Burton. Shall I tell you what it is?"

"Go ahead," Burton answered gloomily.

Mr. Waddington slapped his trousers pocket.

"Before we do another thing," he suggested, "let's go round to the Golden Lion and have just one bottle of beer—just to feel what it's like, eh?"

Burton sprang up.

"By Jove, let's!" he exclaimed. "I've had no breakfast. I'm ravenous. Do they still have that cheese and crusty loaf there?"

Mr. Waddington glanced at the clock.

"It's on by now," he declared. "Come along."

They went out together and trod eagerly yet a trifle sheepishly the very well-known way that led to the Golden Lion. The yellow-haired young lady behind the bar welcomed them with a little cry of astonishment. She tossed her head. Her manner was familiar but was intended to convey some sense of resentment.

"To think of seeing you two again!" she exclaimed. "You, Mr. Waddington, of all gentlemen in the world! Well, I declare!" she went on, holding out her hand across the counter, after having given it a preliminary wipe with a small duster. "Talk about a deserter! Where have you been to every morning, I should like to know?"

"Not anywhere else, my dear," Mr. Waddington asserted, hastily, "that I can assure you. Seem to have lost my taste for beer, or taking anything in the morning lately. Matter of digestion, I suppose. Must obey our doctors, eh? We'll have a tankard each, please. That's right, isn't it, Burton?"

Burton, whose mouth was already full of bread and cheese, nodded. The two men sat down in a little enclosed partition. The yellow-haired young lady leaned across the counter with the air of one willing for conversation.

"Such queer things as I've heard about you, Mr. Waddington," she began. "My! the way people have been talking!"

"That so?" Mr. Waddington muttered. "Wish they'd mind their own business."

"That's too much to expect from folks nowadays," the young lady continued. "Why, there were some saying as you'd come into a fortune and spent all your time in the west-end, some that you'd turned religious, and others that you'd gone a bit dotty. I must say you're looking somehow different, you and Mr. Burton too. It's quite like old times, though, to see you sitting there together. You used to come in after every sale and sit just where you're sitting now and go through the papers. How's the business?"

"Very good," Mr. Waddington admitted. "How have you been getting along, eh?"

The young lady sighed. She rolled her eyes at Mr. Waddington in a manner which was meant to be languishing.

"Very badly indeed," she declared, "thanks to you, you neglectful, ungrateful person! I've heard of fickle men before but I've never met one to come up to one that I could name."

Mr. Waddington moved a little uneasily in his place.

"Been to the theatre lately?" he inquired.

The theatre was apparently a sore point.

"Been to the theatre, indeed!" she repeated. "Why, I refused all the other gentlemen just so as to go with you, and as soon as we got nicely started, why, you never came near again! I've had no chance to go."

Mr. Waddington took out a little book.

"I wonder," he suggested, "if any evening—" "Next Thursday night at seven o'clock, I shall be free," the young lady interrupted promptly. "We'll have a little dinner first, as we used to, and I want to go to the Gaiety. It's lucky you came in," she went on, "for I can assure you that I shouldn't have waited much longer. There are others, you know, that are free enough with their invitations."

She tossed her head. With her hands to the back of her hair she turned round to look at herself for a moment in one of the mirrors which lined the inside of the bar. Burton grinned at his late employer.

"Now you've gone and done it!" he whispered. "Why, you'll have taken a bean before then!"

Mr. Waddington started.

"I'll have to make some excuse," he said.

"You won't be able to," Burton reminded him. "Excuses are not for us, nowadays. You'll have to tell the truth. I'm afraid you've rather put your foot in it."

Mr. Waddington became thoughtful. The young lady, having disposed of some other customers, returned to her place. She rubbed the counter for a few minutes with a duster which hung from the belt around her waist. Then she leaned over once more towards them.

"It's a pity Maud's off duty, Mr. Burton," she remarked. "She's been asking about you pretty nearly every day."

A vision of Maud rose up before Burton's eyes. First of all he shivered. Then in some vague, unwholesome sort of manner he began to find the vision attractive. He found himself actually wishing that she were there—a buxom young woman with dyed hair and sidelong glances, a loud voice, and a distinct fancy for flirtations.

"She is quite well, I hope?" he said.

"Oh, Maudie's all right!" the young lady replied. "Fortunately for her, she's like me—she don't lay too much store on the things you gentlemen say when you come in. Staying away for months at a time!" she continued indignantly. "I'm ashamed of both of you. It's the way we girls always get treated. I shall tell them to lay for you for lunch to-day, anyway."

The two men looked at one another across the round table. Mr. Waddington heaved a sigh.

"I shouldn't bother about that sale, if I were you," Burton whispered hoarsely. "I tell you what it is, I daren't go on like this any longer. I shall do something desperate. This horrible place is getting attractive to me! I shall probably sit here and order more beer and wait till Maud comes; I shall stay to lunch and sit with my arm around her afterwards! I am going to take a bean at once."

Mr. Waddington sighed and produced the snuff-box from his waistcoat pocket. Burton followed suit. The young woman, leaning across the counter, watched them curiously.

"What's that you're taking?" she inquired. "Something for indigestion?"

"Not exactly," Mr. Waddington replied. "It's a little ailment I'm suffering from, and Burton too."

They both swallowed their beans. Burton gave a deep sigh.

"I feel safe again," he murmured. "I am certain that I was on the point of suggesting that she send up for Maud. We might have taken them out together to-night, Mr. Waddington—had dinner at Frascati's, drunk cheap champagne, and gone to a music-hall!"

"Burton," Mr. Waddington said calmly, "I do not for a moment believe that we should so far have forgotten ourselves. I don't know how you are feeling, but the atmosphere of this place is most distasteful to me. These tawdry decorations are positively vicious. The odor, too, is insufferable."

Burton rose hastily to his feet.

"I quite agree with you," he said. "Let us get out as quickly as we can."

"Something," Mr. Waddington went on, "ought to be done to prevent the employment of young women in a public place. It is enough to alter one's whole opinion of the sex to see a brazen-looking creature like that lounging about the bar, and to be compelled to be served by her if one is in need of a little refreshment."

Burton nodded his approbation.

"How we could ever have found our way into the place," he said, "I can't imagine."

"A moment or two ago," Mr. Waddington groaned, "you were thinking of sending up for Maud."

Burton, at this, wiped the perspiration from his forehead.

"Please don't remind me of it," he begged. "Let us get away as quickly as we can."

The young lady leaned over from the bar, holding out a hand, none too clean, on which sparkled several rings.

"Well, you're in a great hurry all at once," she remarked. "Can't you stay a bit longer?"—She glanced at the clock.—"Maud will be down in ten minutes. You're not going away after all this time without leaving a message or something for her, Mr. Burton, surely?"

Burton looked at her across the counter as one might look at some strange creature from a foreign world, a creature to be pitied, perhaps, nothing more.

"I am afraid," he said, "that mine was only a chance visit. Pray remember me to Miss Maud, if you think it would be any satisfaction to her."

The young woman stared at him.

"My, but you are funny!" she declared. "You were always such a one for acting! I'll give her your love, never fear. I shall tell her you'll be round later in the day. On Thursday night, then," she added, turning to Mr. Waddington, "if I don't see you before, and if you really mean you're not going to stay for lunch. I'll meet you at the corner as usual."

Mr. Waddington turned away without apparently noticing the outstretched hand. He raised his hat, however, most politely. "If I should be prevented," he began,—The young woman glared at him.

"Look here, I've had enough of this shilly-shallying!" she exclaimed sharply. "Do you mean taking me out on Thursday or do you not?—because there's a gentleman who comes in here for his beer most every morning who's most anxious I should dine out with him my next night off. I've only to say the word and he'll fetch me in a taxicab. I'm not sure that he hasn't got a motor of his own. No more nonsense, if you please, Mr. Waddington," she continued, shaking out her duster. "Is that an engagement with you on Thursday night, or is it not?"

Mr. Waddington measured with his eye the distance to the door. He gripped Burton's arm and looked over his shoulder.

"It is not," he said firmly.

They left the place a little precipitately. Once in the open air, however, they seemed quickly to recover their equanimity. Burton breathed a deep sigh of relief.

"I must go and change my clothes, Mr. Waddington," he declared. "I don't know how on earth I could have come out looking such a sight. I feel like working, too."

"Such a lovely morning!" Mr. Waddington sighed, gazing up at the sky. "If only one could escape from these hateful streets and get out into the country for a few hours! Have you ever thought of travelling abroad, Burton?"

"Have you?" Burton asked.

Mr. Waddington nodded.

"I have it in my mind at the present moment," he admitted. "Imagine the joy of wandering about in Rome or Florence, say, just looking at the buildings one has heard of all one's life! And the picture galleries—just fancy the picture galleries, Burton! What a dream! Have you ever been to Paris?"

"Never," Burton confessed sadly.

"Nor I," Mr. Waddington continued. "I have been lying awake at nights lately, thinking of Versailles. Why do we waste our time here at all, I wonder, in this ugly little corner of the universe?"

Burton smiled.

"There is something of the hedonist about you, Mr. Waddington," he remarked. "To me these multitudes of people are wonderful. I seem driven always to seek for light in the crowded places."

Mr. Waddington called a taxicab.

"Can I give you a lift?" he asked. "I have no sale until the afternoon. I shall go to one of the galleries. I want to escape from the memory of the last half-hour!"

XX

ANOTHER COMPLICATION

There came a time when Burton finished his novel. He wrapped it up very carefully in brown paper and set out to call upon his friend the sub-editor. He gained his sanctum without any particular trouble and was warmly greeted.

"Why haven't you brought us anything lately?" the sub-editor asked.

Burton tapped the parcel which he was carrying.

"I have written a novel," he said.

The sub-editor was not in the least impressed—in fact he shook his head.

"There are too many novels," he declared.

"I am afraid," Burton replied, "that there will have to be one more, or else I must starve."

"Why have you brought it here, anyhow?"

"I thought you might tell me what to do with it," Burton answered, diffidently.

The sub-editor sighed and drew a sheet of note-paper towards him. He wrote a few lines and put them in an envelope.

"There is a letter of introduction to a publisher," he explained. "Frankly, I don't think it is worth the paper it is written on. Nowadays, novels are published or not, either according to their merit or the possibility of their appealing to the public taste."

Burton looked at the address.

"Thank you very much," he said. "I will take this in myself."

"When are you going to bring us something?" the sub-editor inquired.

"I am going home to try and write something now," Burton replied. "It is either that or the pawnshop."

The sub-editor nodded.

"Novels are all very well for amusement," he said, "but they don't bring in bread and cheese. Come right up to me as soon as you've got something."

Burton left his novel at the address which the sub-editor had given him, and went back to his lodgings. He let himself in with a latchkey.

The caretaker of the floor bustled up to him as he turned towards the door of his room.

"Don't know that I've done right, sir," she remarked, doubtfully. "There was a young person here, waiting about to see you, been waiting the best part of an hour. I let her into your sitting-room."

"Any name?" Burton asked.

The caretaker looked thoughtfully up at the ceiling.

"Said she was your wife, sir. Sorry if I've done wrong. It came over me afterwards that I'd been a bit rash."

Burton threw open the door of his sitting-room and closed it quickly behind him. It was indeed Ellen who was sitting in the most uncomfortable chair, with her arms folded, in an attitude of grim but patient resignation. She was still wearing the hat with the wing, the mauve scarf, the tan shoes, and the velveteen gown. A touch of the Parisienne, however, was supplied to her costume by a black veil dotted over with purple spots. Her taste in perfumes was obviously unaltered.

"Ellen!" he exclaimed.

"Well?" she replied.

As a monosyllabic start to a conversation, Ellen's "Well?" created difficulties. Instead of his demanding an explanation, she was doing it. Burton was conscious that his opening was not brilliant.

"Why, this is quite a surprise!" he said. "I had no idea you were here."

"Dare say not," she answered. "Didn't know I was coming myself till I found myself on the doorstep. Kind of impulse, I suppose. What have you been doing to little Alf?"

Burton looked at her in bewilderment.

"Doing to the boy?" he repeated. "I haven't seen him since I saw you last."

"That's all very well for a tale," Ellen replied, "but you're not going to tell me that he's come into these ways naturally."

"What ways?" Burton exclaimed. "My dear Ellen, you must be a little more explicit. I tell you that I have not seen the child since I was at Garden Green. I am utterly ignorant of anything which may have happened to him."

Ellen remained entirely unconvinced.

"There's things about," she declared, "which I don't understand nor don't want to. First of all you go dotty. Now the same sort of thing seems to have come to little Alf, and what I want to know is what you mean by it? It's all rubbish for you to expect me to believe that he's taken to this naturally."

Burton put his hand to his head for a moment.

"Go on," he said. "Unless you tell me what has happened to Alfred, I cannot even attempt to help you."

"Well, I'll tell you fast enough," Ellen assured him, "though you needn't take that for a proof that I believe what you say. He's been a changed child ever since you were down last. Came home from the school and complained about the other boys not washing properly. Wanted a bath every day, and made me buy him a new toothbrush. Brushes his hair and washes his hands every time he goes out. Took a dislike to his tie and burned it. Plagued me to death till I got him a new suit of clothes—plain, ugly things, too, he would have. He won't have nothing to do with his friends, chucked playing marbles or hopscotch, and goes out in the country, picking flowers. Just to humor him, the first lot he brought home I put in one of those vases that ma brought us from Yarmouth, and what do you think he did?—threw the vase out of the window and bought with his own pocket money a plain china bowl."

Burton listened in blank amazement. As yet the light had not come.

"Go on," he murmured. "Anything else?"

"Up comes his master a few days ago," Ellen continued. "Fairly scared me to death. Said the boy showed signs of great talent in drawing. Talent in drawing, indeed! I'll give him talent! Wanted me to have him go to night school and pay for extra lessons. Said he thought the boy would turn out an artist. Nice bit of money there is in that!"

"What did you tell him?" Burton asked.

"I told him to stop putting silly ideas into the child's head," Ellen replied. "We don't want to make no artist of Alfred. Into an office he's got to go as soon as he's passed his proper standard, and that's what I told his schoolmaster. Calling Alf a genius, indeed!"

"Is this all that's troubling you?" Burton inquired calmly.

"All?" Ellen cried. "Bless my soul, as though it wasn't enough! A nice harmless boy as ever was until that day that you came down. You don't seem to understand. He's like a little old man. Chooses his words, corrects my grammar, keeps himself so clean you can almost smell the soap. What I say is that it isn't natural in a child of his age."

Burton smiled.

"Well, really," he said, "I don't see anything to worry about in what you have told me."

"Don't you!" Ellen replied. "Well, just you listen to me and answer my question. I left Alf alone with you while I changed my—while I looked after the washing the day you came, and what I want to know is, did you give him one of those things that you talked to me about?"

"I certainly did not," Burton answered.

Then a light broke in upon him. Ellen saw the change in his face.

"Well, what is it?" she asked sharply. "I can see you know all about it."

"There were the two beans you threw out of the window," he said. "He must have picked up one."

"Beans, indeed!" Ellen replied, scornfully. "Do you mean to tell me that a bean would work all this mischief in the child?"

"I happen to know that it would."

"Comes of picking up things in the street!" Ellen exclaimed. "I'll give it him when I get back, I will!"

"You must forgive me," Burton said, "but I really don't see what you have to complain about. From what you tell me, I should consider the boy very much improved."

"Improved!" Ellen repeated. "An unnatural little impudent scallywag of a child! You don't think I want a schoolmaster in knickerbockers about the place all the time? Found fault with my clothes yesterday, hid some of the ornaments in the parlor, and I caught him doing a sketch of a woman the other day with not a shred of clothes on. Said it was a copy of some statue in the library. It may be your idea of how a boy nine years old should go on, but it isn't mine, and that's straight."

Burton sighed.

"My dear Ellen," he said, "we do not look at this matter from the same point of view, but fortunately as you will say, unfortunately from my point of view, the change in Alfred is not likely to prove lasting. You will find in another few weeks that he will be himself again."

"Don't believe it," Ellen declared. "He's as set in his ways now as a little old man."

Burton shook his head.

"It won't last, I know it."

"Lasts with you all right!" she snapped.

Burton opened his little silver box.

"It lasts with me only as long as these little beans last," he replied. "You see, I have only two left. When they are gone, I shall be back again."

"If you think," Ellen exclaimed, "that you're going to march into Clematis Villa just when you feel like it, and behave as though nothing has happened, all I can say, my man, is that you're going to be disappointed! You've kept away so long you can keep away for good. We can do without you, me and Alf."

Burton still held the box in his hand.

"I suppose," he ventured slowly, "I couldn't persuade you to take one?"

Ellen rose to her feet. She threw the scarf around her neck, buttoned her gloves, and shook out her skirt. She picked up the satchel which she had been carrying and prepared to depart.

"If you say anything more to me about your beastly beans," she said, "I'll lose my temper, and that's straight. Can you tell me how to bring little Alf to himself again? That's all I want to know."

"Time will do that, unfortunately," Burton assured her. "Where is he this afternoon?

"It's his half-holiday," Ellen replied, in a tone of disgust, "and where do you think he's gone? Gone to a museum to look at some statues! The schoolmaster called for him. They've gone off together. All I can say is that if he don't turn natural again before long, you can have him. He don't belong to me no longer."

"I am willing to take the responsibility," Burton replied, "if it is necessary. Will you let me give you some tea?"

"I want nothing from you except my weekly money that the law provides for," Ellen answered fiercely. "You can keep your tea. And mind what I say, too. It's no use coming down to Clematis Villa and talking about the effect of the bean having worn off and being yourself again. You seem pretty comfortable here and you can stay here until I'm ready for you. Oh, bother holding the door open!" she added, angrily. "I hate such tricks! Get out of the way and let me pass. I can let myself out. More fool me for coming! I might have known you'd have nothing sensible to say."

"I'm afraid," Burton admitted, "that we do rather look at this matter from different points of view, but, as I told you before, you will find very soon that Alfred will be just the same as he used to be."

"If he don't alter," Ellen declared, looking back from the door, "you'll find him here one day by Carter Patterson's, with a label around his neck. I'm not one for keeping children about the place that know more than their mothers. I give him another three weeks, and not a day longer. What do you think was the last thing he did? Went and had his hair cut—wanted to get rid of his curl, he said."

"I can't blame him for that," Burton remarked, smiling. "I never thought it becoming. Will you shake hands, Ellen, before you go?"

"I won't!" she replied, drawing up her skirt in genteel fashion. "I want nothing to do with you. Only, if he don't alter, well, just you look out, for you'll find him on your doorstep."

She departed in a "Lily of the Valley" scent and little fragments of purple fluff. Burton threw himself into an easy-chair.

"If one could only find the tree," he muttered to himself. "What a life for the boy! Poor little chap!"

XXI

An Amazing Transformation

The novel which was to bring immortal fame and, incidentally, freedom from all financial responsibilities, to Burton, came back within a week, with a polite note which he was at first inclined to accept as some consolation until he found that it was stereotyped. Within a few hours it was despatched to another firm of publishers, taken at random from the advertisement columns of the Times. An hour or two afterwards Alfred arrived, with no label around his neck, but a veritable truant. Of the two he was the more self-possessed as he greeted his amazed parent.

"I am sorry if you are angry about my coming, father," he said, a little tremulously. "Something seems to have happened to mother during the last few days. Everything that I do displeases her."

"I am not angry," Burton declared, after a moment's amazed silence. "The only thing is," he added, glancing helplessly around, "I don't know what to do with you. I have no servants here and only my one little bed."

The child smiled. He appeared to consider these matters unimportant.

"You eat things sometimes, I suppose, daddy?" he said, apologetically. "I left home before breakfast this morning and it took me some time to find my way here."

"Sit down for five minutes," Burton directed him, "and I'll take you out somewhere."

Burton was glad to get into the privacy of his small bedroom and sit down for a moment. The thing was amazing enough when it had happened to himself. It was, perhaps, more amazing still to watch its effect upon Mr. Waddington. But certainly this was the most astounding development of all! The child was utterly transformed. There was no sign of his mother's hand upon his clothes, his neatly brushed hair or his shiny face. His eyes, too, seemed to have grown bigger. Alfred had been a vulgar little boy, addicted to slang and immoderately fond of noisy games. Burton tried to call him back to his mind. It was impossible to connect him in any way with the child whom, through a crack in the door, he could see standing upon a chair the better to scrutinize closely the few engravings which hung upon the wall. Without a doubt, a new responsibility in life had arrived. To meet it, Burton had a little less than two pounds, and the weekly money to send to Ellen within a few days. He took Alfred out to luncheon.

"I am afraid," he said, beginning their conversation anew, "that even if I am able to keep you with me for a short time, you will find it exceedingly dull."

"I do not mind being dull in the least, father," the boy replied. "Mother is always wanting me to play silly games out in the street, with boys whom I don't like at all."

"I used to see you playing with them often," his father reminded him.

The child looked puzzled. He appeared to be trying to recollect something.

"Daddy, some things in the world seem so funny," he said, thoughtfully. "I know that I used to like to play with Teddy Miles and Dick, hopscotch and marbles, and relievo. Relievo is a very rough game, and marbles makes one very dirty and dusty. Still, I know that I used to like to play those games. I don't want to now a bit. I would rather read. If you are busy, daddy, I shan't mind a bit. Please don't think that you will have to play with me. I want to read, I shall be quite happy reading all the time. Mr. Denschem has given me a list of books. Perhaps you have some of them. If not, couldn't we get some out of a library?"

Burton looked at the list which the boy produced, and groaned to himself.

"My dear Alfred," he protested, "these books are for almost grown-up people."

The boy smiled confidently.

"Mr. Denschem gave me the list, father," he repeated simply.

After lunch, Burton took the boy round to Mr. Waddington's office. Mr. Waddington was deep in a book of engravings which he had just purchased. He welcomed Burton warmly and gazed with surprise at the child.

"Alfred," his father directed, "go and sit in that easy-chair for a few minutes. I want to talk to Mr. Waddington."

The child obeyed at once. His eyes, however, were longingly fixed upon the book of engravings.

"Perhaps you would like to have a look at these?" Mr. Waddington suggested.

Alfred held out his hands eagerly.

"Thank you very much," he said. "It is very kind of you. I am very fond of this sort of picture."

Burton took Mr. Waddington by the arm and led him out into the warehouse.

"Whose child is that?" the latter demanded curiously.

"Mine," Burton groaned. "Can you guess what has happened?"

Mr. Waddington looked puzzled.

"You remember the day I went down to Garden Green? You gave me two beans to give to Ellen and the child. It was before we knew that their action was not permanent."

"I remember quite well," Mr. Waddington confessed.

"You remember I told you that Ellen threw them both into the street? A man who was wheeling a fruit barrow picked up one. I told you about that?"

"Yes!"

"This child picked up the other," Burton declared, solemnly.

Mr. Waddington stared at him blankly. "You don't mean to tell me," he said, "that this is the ill-dressed, unwashed, unmannerly little brat whom your wife brought into the office one day, and who turned the ink bottles upside down and rubbed the gum on his hands?"

"This is the child," Burton admitted.

"God bless my soul!" Mr. Waddington muttered.

They sat down together on the top of a case. Neither of them found words easy.

"He's taken to drawing," Burton continued slowly, "hates the life at home, goes out for walks with the schoolmaster. He's got a list of books to read—classics every one of them."

"Poor little fellow!" Mr. Waddington said to himself. "And to think that in three weeks or a month—"

"And in the meantime," Burton interrupted, "here he is on my hands. He's run away from home—as I did. I don't wonder at it. What do you advise me to do, Mr. Waddington?"

"What can you do?" Mr. Waddington replied. "You must keep him until—"

"Upon children," Burton said thoughtfully, "the effect may be more lasting. No news, I suppose, of the tree?"

Mr. Waddington shook his head sorrowfully. "I've had a private detective now working ever since that day," he declared. "The man thinks me, of course, a sort of lunatic, but I have made it worth his while to find it. I should think that every child in the neighborhood has been interviewed. What about the novel?"

"Come back from the publishers," Burton replied. "I have sent it away to some one else."

Mr. Waddington looked at him compassionately.

"You were relying upon that, were you not?"

"Entirely," Burton admitted. "If I don't earn some money before Saturday, I shan't know how to send the three pounds to Ellen."

"You had better," Mr. Waddington said gently, accept a trifling loan.

"Not if I can help it," Burton answered, hastily. "Thank you all the same, Mr. Waddington, but I would rather not. We will see what happens. I am going back now to try and write something."

They returned to the office. Burton pointed towards the easy-chair. "Look!"

Mr. Waddington nodded. Alfred had propped up the book of engravings before him, was holding a sheet of paper on the blotting-pad, and with a pencil was intently copying one of the heads. They crossed the room and peered over his shoulder. For an untrained child it was an amazing piece of work.

"It is a Botticelli head," Mr. Waddington whispered. "Look at the outline."

The boy glanced up and saw them standing there. He excused himself gracefully.

"You don't mind, sir, do you?" he asked Mr. Waddington. "I took a sheet of paper from your office. This head was so wonderful, I wanted to carry away something that would remind me of it."

"If you like," Mr. Waddington offered, "I will lend you the book of engravings. Then when your father is busy you could make copies of some that please you."

The boy's cheeks were pink and his eyes soft.

"How lovely!" he exclaimed. "Father, may I have it?"

He left the office with the book clasped under his arm. On the way home, Burton bought him some drawing-paper and pencils. For the remainder of the afternoon they both worked in silence. Of the two, the boy was the more completely engrossed. Towards five o'clock Burton made tea, which they took together. Alfred first carefully washed his hands, and his manners at table were irreproachable. Burton began to feel uncomfortable. He felt that the spirit of some older person had come to him in childlike guise. There was so little to connect this boy with the Alfred of his recollections. In looking over his work, too, Burton was conscious of an almost awed sense of a power in this child's fingers which could have been directed by no ordinary inspiration. From one to another of those prints, the outlines of which he had committed to paper, the essential quality of the work, the underlying truth, seemed inevitably to be reproduced. There were mistakes of perspective and outline, crudities, odd little touches, and often a failure of proportion, and yet that one fact always remained. The meaning of the picture was there. The only human note about the child seemed to be that, looking at him shortly after tea-time, Burton discovered that he had fallen asleep in his chair.

Burton took up his hat and stole softly out of the room. As quickly as he could, he made his way to the offices of the Piccadilly Gazette and sought his friend the sub-editor. The sub-editor greeted him with a nod.

"Heard about your novel yet?" he inquired.

"I had it back this morning," his caller replied. "I have sent it away somewhere else. I have written you a little study of 'The Children of London.' I hope you will like it."

The sub-editor nodded and glanced it through. He laid it down by his side and for the first time there seemed to be a shadow of hesitation in his tone.

"Don't force yourself, Burton," he advised, looking curiously at his contributor. "We will use this in a day or two. You can apply at the cashier's office for your cheque when you like. But if you don't mind my saying so, there are little touches here, repetitions, that might be improved, I think."

Burton thanked him and went home with money in his pocket. He undressed the boy, who sleepily demanded a bath, put him to sleep in his own bed, and threw himself into an easy-chair. It was late, but he had not troubled to light a lamp. He sat for hours looking out into the shadows. A new responsibility, indeed, had come into life. He was powerless to grapple with it. The grotesqueness of the situation appalled him. How could he plan or dream like other men when the measure of the child's existence, as of his own, could be counted by weeks? For the first time since his emancipation he looked back into the past without a shudder. If one had realized, if one had only taken a little pains, would it not have been possible to have escaped from the life of bondage by less violent but more permanent means? It was only the impulse which was lacking. He sat dreaming there until he fell into a deep sleep.

E. PHILLIPS OPPENHEIM

XXII

Doubts

M r. Bomford in his town clothes was a strikingly adequate reflection of the fashion of the times. From the tips of his patent boots, his neatly tied black satin tie, his waistcoat with its immaculate white slip, to his glossy silk hat, he was an entirely satisfactory reproduction. The caretaker who admitted him to Burton's rooms sighed as she let him in. He represented exactly her ideal of a gentleman.

"Mr. Burton and the little boy are both in the sitting-room, sir," she announced, opening the door. "A gentleman to see you, sir."

Burton looked up from his writing-table for a moment somewhat vaguely. Mr. Bomford, who had withdrawn his glove, held out his hand.

"I trust, Mr. Burton, that you have not entirely forgotten me," he said. "I had the pleasure of dining with you a short time ago at Professor Cowper's. You will doubtless remember our conversation?"

Burton welcomed his visitor civilly and motioned him to a seat. He was conscious of feeling a little disturbed. Mr. Bomford brought him once more into touch with memories which were ever assailing him by night and by day.

"I have taken the liberty of calling upon you, Mr. Burton," the newcomer continued, setting down his silk hat upon a corner of the table, and lifting his coat-tails preparatory to sinking into a chair, "because I believe that in the excitement of our conversation a few nights ago, we did not do adequate justice to the sentiments which—er—provoked our offer to you."

Mr. Bomford sat down with the air of a man who has spoken well. He was thoroughly pleased with his opening sentence.

"It did not occur to me," Burton replied, "that there was any possibility of misunderstanding anything you or Professor Cowper said. Still, it is very kind of you to come and see me."

Alfred, who was drawing in colored chalks at the other end of the room, rose up and approached his father.

"Would you like me to go into the other room, father?" he asked. "I can leave my work quite easily for a time, and I have several books there."

Mr. Bomford screwed an eyeglass into his eye and looked across at the child.

"What an extraordinarily—forgive my remark, Mr. Burton—but what an extraordinarily well-behaved child! Is it possible that this is your boy?"

Alfred turned his head and there was no doubt about the relationship. He, too, possessed the deep-set eyes with their strange, intense glow, the quivering mouth, the same sensitiveness of outline.

"Yes, this is my son," Burton admitted, quietly. "Go and shake hands with Mr. Bomford, Alfred."

The child crossed the room and held out his hand with grave self-possession.

"It is very kind of you to come and see father," he said. "I am afraid that sometimes he is very lonely here. I will go away and leave you to talk."

Mr. Bomford fumbled in his pocket.

"Dear me!" he exclaimed. "Dear me! Ah, here is a half-crown! You must buy some chocolates or something to-morrow, young man. Or a gun, eh? Can one buy a gun for half-a-crown?"

Alfred smiled at him.

"It is very kind of you, sir," he said slowly. "I do not care for chocolate or guns, but if my father would allow me to accept your present, I should like very much to buy a larger drawing block."

Mr. Bomford looked at the child and looked at his father.

"Buy anything you like," he murmured weakly,—"anything you like at all."

The child glanced towards his father. Burton nodded.

"Certainly you may keep the half-crown, dear," he assented. "It is one of the privileges of your age to accept presents. Now run along into the other room, and I will come in and fetch you presently."

The child held out his hand once more to Mr. Bomford.

"It is exceedingly kind of you to give me this, sir," he said. "I can assure you that the drawing block will be a great pleasure to me."

He withdrew with a little nod and a smile. Mr. Bomford watched him pass into the inner room, with his mouth open.

"God bless my soul, Burton!" he exclaimed. "What an extraordinary child!"

Burton laughed, a little hoarsely.

"A few weeks ago," he said, "that boy was running about the streets with greased hair, a butcher's curl, a soiled velveteen suit, a filthy lace collar, dirty hands, torn stockings, playing disreputable games with all the urchins of the neighborhood. He murdered the Queen's English every time he spoke, and spent his pennies on things you suck. His mother threw two of the beans I had procured with great difficulty for them both into the street. He picked one up and ate it—a wretched habit of his. You see the result."

Mr. Bomford sat quite still and breathed several times before he spoke. It was a sign with him of most intense emotion.

"Mr. Burton," he declared, "if this is true, that child is even a greater testimony to the efficacy of your—your beans, than you yourself."

"There is no doubt," Burton agreed, "that the change is even greater."

There was a knock at the door. Burton, with a word of excuse, crossed the room to open it. The postman stood there with a packet. It was his novel returned once more. He threw it on to a table in the corner and returned to his place.

"Mr. Burton," his visitor continued, "for the first time in my life— and I may say that I have been accustomed to public speaking and am considered to have a fair choice of words—for the first time in my life I confess that I find myself in trouble as to exactly how to express myself. I want to convince you. I am myself entirely and absolutely convinced as to the justice of the cause I plead. I want you to reconsider your decision of the other night."

Burton shook his head.

"I am afraid," he said, uneasily, "that that is not possible."

Mr. Bomford cleared his throat. He was only externally a fool.

"Mr. Burton," he declared, "you are an artist. Your child has the makings of a great artist. Have you no desire to travel? Have you no desire to see the famous picture galleries and cities of the Continent, cities which have been the birthplaces of the men whose works you and your son in days to come will regard with so much reverence?"

"I should like to travel very much indeed," Burton admitted.

"It is the opportunity to travel which we offer you," Mr. Bomford reminded him. "It is the opportunity to surround yourself with beautiful objects, the opportunity to make your life free from anxieties, a cultured phase of being during which, removed from all material cares, you can— er—develop yourself and the boy in any direction you choose."

Mr. Bomford stopped and coughed. Again he was pleased with himself.

"Money is only vulgar," he went on, "to vulgar minds. And remember this—that underlying the whole thing there is Truth. The beans which you and the boy have eaten do contain something of the miraculous. Those same constituents would be blended in the preparation which we shall offer to the public. Have you no faith in them? Why should you not believe it possible that the ingredients which have made so great a change in you and that child, may not influence for the better the whole world of your fellow-creatures? Omit for a moment the reflection that you yourself would benefit so much by the acceptance of my offer. Consider only your fellow human creatures. Don't you realize—can't you see that in acceding to our offer you will be acting the part of a philanthropist?"

"Mr. Bomford," Burton said, leaning a little forward, "in all your arguments you forget one thing. My stock of these beans is already perilously low. When they are gone, I remain no more what I hope and believe I am at the present moment. Once more I revert to the impossible: I become the auctioneer's clerk—a commonplace, material, vulgar, objectionable little bounder, whose doings and feelings I sometimes dimly remember. Can't you imagine what sort of use a person like that would make of wealth? In justice to him, in justice to the myself of the future, I cannot place such temptations in his way."

Mr. Bomford was staggered.

"I find it hard to follow you," he admitted. "You will not accept my offer because you are afraid that when the effect of these beans has worn off, you will misuse the wealth which will come to you—is that it?"

"That is the entire truth," Burton confessed.

"Have you asked yourself," Mr. Bomford demanded, impressively, "whether you have a right to treat your other self in this fashion? Your other self will assuredly resent it, if you retain your memory. Your other self would hate your present self for its short-sighted, quixotic folly. I tell you frankly that you have not the right to treat your coming self in this way. Consider! Wealth does not inevitably vulgarize. On the contrary, it takes you away from the necessity of associating with people calculated to depress and cramp your life. There are many points of view which I am sure you have not adequately considered. Take the case of our friend Professor Cowper, for instance. He is a poor man with a scientific hobby in which he is burning to indulge. Why deprive him of the opportunity? There is his daughter—"

"I will reconsider the matter," Burton interrupted, hastily. "I cannot say more than that."

E. PHILLIPS OPPENHEIM

Mr. Bomford signified his satisfaction.

"I am convinced," he said, "that you will come around to our way of thinking. I proceed now to the second reason of my visit to you this afternoon. Professor Cowper and his daughter are doing me the honor to dine with me to-night at the Milan. I beg that you will join us."

Burton sat for some time without reply. For a moment the strong wave of humanity which swept up from his heart and set his pulses leaping, set the music beating in the air, terrified him. Surely this could mean but one thing! He waited almost in agony for the thoughts which might fill his brain.

"Miss Cowper," Mr. Bomford continued, "has been much upset since your hasty departure from Leagate. She is conscious of some mistake— some foolish speech."

Burton drew a little sigh of relief. After all, what he had feared was not coming. He saw the flaw, he felt even now the revulsion of feeling with which her words had inspired him. Yet the other things remained. She was still wonderful. It was still she who was the presiding genius of that sentimental garden.

"You are very kind," he murmured.

"We shall expect you," Mr. Bomford declared, "at a quarter past eight this evening."

XXIII

CONDEMNED!

To Burton, who was in those days an epicure in sensations, there was something almost ecstatic in the pleasure of that evening. They dined at a little round table in the most desirable corner of the room—the professor and Edith, Mr. Bomford and himself. The music of one of the most famous orchestras in Europe alternately swelled and died away, always with the background of that steady hum of cheerful conversation. It was his first experience of a restaurant de luxe. He looked about him in amazed wonder. He had expected to find himself in a palace of gilt, to find the prevailing note of the place an unrestrained and inartistic gorgeousness. He found instead that the decorations everywhere were of spotless white, the whole effect one of cultivated and restful harmony. The glass and linen on the table were perfect. There was nowhere the slightest evidence of any ostentation. Within a few feet of him, separated only by that little space of tablecloth and a great bowl of pink roses, sat Edith, dressed as he had never seen her before, a most becoming flush upon her cheeks, a new and softer brilliancy in her eyes, which seemed always to be seeking his. They drank champagne, to the taste and effects of which he was as yet unaccustomed. Burton felt its inspiring effect even though he himself drank little.

The conversation was always interesting. The professor talked of Assyria, and there was no man who had had stranger experiences. He talked with the eloquence and fervor of a man who speaks of things which have become a passion with him; so vividly, indeed, that more than once he seemed to carry his listeners with him, back through the ages, back into actual touch with the life of thousands of years ago, which he described with such full and picturesque detail. Not at any time during the dinner was the slightest allusion made to that last heated interview which had taken place between the three men. Even when they sat out in the palm court afterwards, and smoked and listened to the band and watched the people, Mr. Bomford only distantly alluded to it.

"I want to ask you, Mr. Burton," he said, "what you think of your surroundings—of the restaurant and your neighbors on every side?"

"The restaurant is very beautiful," Burton admitted. "The whole place seems delightful. One can only judge of the people by their appearance. That, at any rate, is in their favor."

Mr. Bomford nodded approvingly.

"I will admit, Mr. Burton," he continued, leaning a little towards him, "that one of my objects in asking you to dine this evening, apart from the pleasure of your company, was to prove to you the truth of one of my remarks the other evening—that the expenditure of money need not necessarily be associated with vulgarity. This is a restaurant which only the rich could afford to patronize save occasionally, yet you see for yourself that the prominent note here is a subdued and artistic tastefulness. The days of loud colors and of the flamboyant life are past. Money to-day is the handmaiden to culture."

Exceedingly pleased with his speech, Mr. Bomford leaned back in his chair and lighted a half-crown cigar. Presently, without any visible co-operation on their part, a little scheme was carried into effect by the professor and Mr. Bomford. The latter rose and crossed to the other side of the room to speak to some friends. A few moments later he beckoned to the professor. Edith and Burton were alone. She drew a deep sigh of relief and turned towards him as though expecting him to say something. Burton, however, was silent. He had never seen her quite like this. She wore a plain white satin dress and a string of pearls about her neck, which he saw for the first time entirely exposed. The excitement of the evening had brought a delicate flush to her face; the blue in her eyes was more wonderful here, even, than out in the sunlight. Amid many toilettes of more complicated design, the exquisite and entire simplicity of her gown and hair and ornaments was delightful.

"You are quiet this evening," she whispered. "I wish I could know what you are thinking of all the time."

"There is nothing in my thoughts or in my heart," he answered, "which I would not tell you if I could. Evenings like this, other evenings which you and I have spent together in still more beautiful places, have been like little perfect epochs in an imperfect life. Yet all the time one is haunted. I am haunted here to-night, even, as I sit by your side. I move through life a condemned man. I know it for I have proved it. Before very long the man whom you know, who sits by your side at this moment, who is your slave, dear, must pass."

"You can never altogether change," she murmured.

His hands clasped the small silver box in his pocket.

"In a few months," he said hoarsely, "unless we can find the missing plant, I shall be again the common little clerk who came and peered over your hedge at you in the summer."

She smiled a little incredulously.

"Even when you tell me so," she insisted, "I cannot believe it."

He drew his chair closer to hers. He looked around him nervously, the horror was in his eyes.

"Since I saw you last," he continued, "I have been very nearly like it. I couldn't travel alone, I bought silly comic papers, I played nap with young men who talked of nothing but their 'shop' and their young ladies. I have been to a public-house, drunk beer, and shaken hands with the barmaid. I was even disappointed when one of them—a creature with false hair, a loud, rasping voice and painted lips—was not there. Just in time I took one of my beans and became myself again, but Edith, I have only two more. When they are gone there is an end of me. That is why I sit here by your side at this moment and feel myself a condemned man. I think that when I feel the change coming I shall throw myself over into the river. I could not bear the other life again!"

"Absurd!" she declared.

"If I believed," he went on, "that I could carry with me across that curious boundary enough of decency, enough of my present feelings, to keep us wholly apart, I would be happier. It is one of the terrors of my worst moments when I think that in the months or years to come I may again be tempted—no, not I, but Alfred Burton of Garden Green may be tempted—to look once more across the hedge for you."

She smiled reassuringly at him.

"You do not terrify me in the least. I shall ask you in to tea."

He groaned.

"My speech will be Cockney and my manners a little forward," he said, in a tone of misery. "If I see your piano I shall want to vamp."

"I think," she murmured, "that for the sake of the Alfred Burton who is sitting by my side to-night, I shall still be kind to you. Perhaps you will not need my sympathy, though. Perhaps you will adapt yourself wholly to your new life when the time comes."

He shook his head.

"There are cells in one's memory," he muttered. "I don't understand—I don't know how they get there—but don't you remember that time last summer when I was picnicking with my common friends? We were drinking beer out of a stone jug, we were singing vulgar songs, we

E. PHILLIPS OPPENHEIM

were revelling in the silly puerilities of a bank holiday out of doors. And I saw your face and something came to me. I saw for a moment over the wall. Dear, I am very sure that if I go back there will be times when I shall see over the wall, and my heart will ache and the whole taste of life will be like dust between my teeth."

She leaned towards him.

"It is your fault if I say this," she whispered. "It is you yourself who have prepared the way. Why not make sure of riches? The world can give so much to the rich. You can buy education, manners, taste. Anything, surely, would be better than taking up the life of an auctioneer's clerk once more? With riches you can at least get away from the most oppressive forms of vulgarity."

"I wish I could believe it," he replied. "The poor man is, as a rule, natural. The rich man has the taste of other things on his palate; he has looked over the wrong wall, he apes what he sees in the wrong garden."

"Not always," she pleaded. "Don't you believe that something will remain of these splendid months of yours—some will power, some faint impulse towards the choicer ways of life? Oh, it really must be so!" she went on, more confidently. "I am sure of it. I think of you as you are now, how carefully you control even your emotions, how sensitive you always are in your speech, and I know that you could never revert entirely to those other days. You may slip back, and slip back a long way, but there would always be something to keep you from the depths."

Her eyes were glowing. Her fingers deliberately touched his for a moment.

"It is wonderful to hope that it may be so," he sighed. "Even as I sit here and remember that awful picnic party, I remember, too, that something drew me a little away from the others to gaze into your garden and at you. There was something, even then, which kept me from being with them while I looked, and I know that at that moment, at the moment I looked up and met your eyes, I know that there was no vulgar thought in my heart."

"Dear," she said, "with every word you make me the more inclined to persist. I honestly believe that father and Mr. Bomford are right. It is your duty. You owe it to yourself to accept their offer."

He sat for several minutes without speech.

"If I could only make you understand!" he went on at last. "Somehow, I feel as though it would be making almost a vulgar use of something which is to me divine. These strange little things which Mr. Bomford would have me barter for money, brought me out of the unclean world and showed me how beautiful life might be—showed me, indeed, what beauty really is. There is no religion has ever brought such joy to the heart of a man, nor any love, nor any of the great passions of the world have opened such gates as they have done for me. You can't imagine what the hideous life is like—the life of vulgar days, of ugly surroundings, the dull and ceaseless trudge side by side with the multitude across the sterile plain, without the power to raise one's eyes, without the power to stretch out one's arms and feel the throb of freedom in one's pulses. If I die to-morrow, I shall at least have lived for a little time, thanks to these. Can you wonder that I think of them with reverence? Yet you ask me to make use of one of them to help launch upon the world a patent food, something built upon the credulity of fools, something whose praises must be sung in blatant advertisements, desecrating the pages of magazines, gaping from the hoardings, thrust inside the chinks of human simplicity by the art of the advertising agent. Edith, it is a hard thing, this. Do try and realize how hard it is. If there be anything in the world divine, if there be anything sacred at all, anything to lift one from the common way, it is what you ask me to sacrifice."

"You are such a sentimentalist, dear," she whispered. "You need have no share in the commercial part of this. The money can simply keep you while you write, or help you to travel."

"It will lead that other fellow," he groaned, "into no end of mischief."

The professor and Mr. Bomford returned. They talked for a little time together and then the party broke up. As they waited for Edith to get her cloak, Burton spoke the few words which they were both longing to hear.

"Mr. Bomford," he announced, "and professor, I should like to see you to-morrow. I am going to think over this matter to-night once more. It is very possible that I may see my way clear to do as you ask."

"Mr. Burton, sir," the professor said, grasping his hand, "I congratulate you. I felt sure that your common sense would assert itself. Let me assure you of one thing, too. Indirectly you will be the cause of marvelous discoveries, enlightening discoveries, being made as to the source of some of that older civilization which still bewilders the student of prehistoric days."

Mr. Bomford had less to say but he was quite as emphatic.

"If you only think hard enough, Mr. Burton," he declared, "you can't make a mistake."

He saw them into the motor, Edith in a cloak of lace which made her seem like some dainty, fairylike creature as she stepped from the pavement into a corner of the landaulette. Afterwards, he walked with uplifted heart through the streets and back to his rooms. He let himself in with a mechanical turn of the key. On the threshold he stood still in sudden amazement. The lights were all turned on, the room was in rank disorder. Simmering upon the hearth were the remains of his novel; upset upon the table several pots of paint. Three chairs were lashed together with a piece of rope. On a fourth sat Alfred, cracking a home-made whip. His hands were covered with coal-dust, traces of which were smeared upon his cheeks. There were spots of ink all down his clothes, his eyes seemed somehow to have crept closer together. There were distinct signs of a tendency on the part of his hair to curl over a certain spot on his forehead. He looked at his father like a whipped hound but he said never a word.

"What on earth have you been doing, Alfred?" Burton faltered.

The boy dropped his whip and put his finger in his mouth. He was obviously on the point of howling.

"You left me here all alone," he said, in an aggrieved tone. "There was no one to play with, nothing to do. I want to go back to mother; I want Ned and Dick to play with. Don't want to stop here any longer."

He began to howl. Burton looked around once more at the scene of his desolation. He moved to the fireplace and gazed down at the charred remnants of his novel. The boy continued to howl.

XXIV

Menatogen, the Mind Food

I t had been a dinner of celebration. The professor had ransacked his cellar and produced his best wine. He had drunk a good deal of it himself—so had Mr. Bomford. A third visitor, Mr. Horace Bunsome, a company promoter from the city, had been even more assiduous in his attentions to a particular brand of champagne.

Burton had been conscious of a sense of drifting. The more human side of him was paramount. The dinner was perfect; the long, low dining-room, with its bowls of flowers and quaint decorations, delightful; the wine and food the best of their sort. Edith, looking like an exquisite picture, was sitting by his side. After all, if the end of things were to come this way, what did it matter? She had no eyes for any one else, her fingers had touched his more than once. The complete joy of living was in his pulses. He, too, had yielded to the general spirit.

Edith left them late and reluctantly. Then the professor raised his glass. There was an unaccustomed color in his parchment-white cheeks. His spectacles were sitting at a new angle, his black tie had wandered from its usual precise place around to the side of his neck.

"Let us drink," he exclaimed, "to the new company! To the new Mind Food, to the new scientific diet of the coming century! Let us drink to ourselves, the pioneers of this wonderful discovery, the manufacturers and owners-to-be of the new food, the first of its kind created and designed to satisfy the moral appetite."

"We'll have a little of that in the prospectus," Mr. Horace Bunsome remarked, taking out his notebook. "It sounds mighty good, professor."

"It sounds good because it is true, sir," Mr. Cowper asserted, a little severely. "Your services, Mr. Bunsome, are necessary to us, but I beg that you will not confound the enterprise in which you will presently find yourself engaged, with any of the hazardous, will-o'-the-wisp undertakings which spring up day by day, they tell me, in the city, and which owe their very existence and such measure of success as they may achieve, to the credulity of fools. Let me impress upon you, Mr. Bunsome, that you are, on this occasion, associated with a genuine and marvelous discovery—the scientific discovery, sir, of the age. You are going to be one of those who will offer to the world a genuine—an absolutely genuine tonic to the moral system."

Mr. Bunsome nodded approvingly.

"The more I hear you talk," he declared, "the more I like the sound of it. People are tired of brain foods and nerve foods. A food for the moral self! Professor, you're a genius."

"I am nothing of the sort, sir," the professor answered. "My share in this is trifling. The discovery is the discovery of our friend here," he continued, indicating Burton. "The idea of exploiting it is the idea of Mr. Bomford. . . My young friend Burton, you, at least, must rejoice with us to-night. You must rejoice, in your heart, that our wise counsels have prevailed. You must feel that you have done a great and a good action in sharing this inheritance of yours with millions of your fellow-creatures."

Burton leaned a little forward in his place.

"Professor," he said, "remember that there are only two small beans, each less than the size of a sixpence, which I have handed over to you. As to the qualities which they possess, there is no shadow of doubt about them for I myself am a proof. Yet you take one's breath away with your schemes. How could you, out of two beans, provide a food for millions?"

The professor smiled.

"Science will do it, my dear Mr. Burton," he replied, with some note of patronage in his tone, "science, the highways of which to you are an untrodden road. I myself am a chemist. I myself, before I felt the call of Assyria, have made discoveries not wholly unimportant. This afternoon I spent four hours in my laboratory with one of your beans. I tell you frankly that I have discovered constituents in that small article which absolutely stupefy me, qualities which no substance on earth that I know of, in the vegetable or mineral world, possesses. Yet within a week, the chemist whom I have engaged to come to my assistance and I will assuredly have resolved that little bean into a definite formula. When we have done that, the rest is easy. Its primary constituents will form the backbone of our new food. If we are only able to reproduce them in trifling quantities, then we must add a larger proportion of some harmless and negative substance. The matter is simple."

"No worry about that, that I can see," Mr. Bunsome remarked. "So long as we have this testimony of Mr. Burton's, and the professor's introduction and explanation, we don't really need the bean at all. We've only got to print his story, get hold of some tasteless sort of stuff that no one can exactly analyze, and the whole thing's done so far as we are concerned. Of course, whether it takes on or not with the public is always a bit of a risk, but the risk doesn't lie with us to control. It depends entirely upon the advertisements. If we are able to engage Rentoul, and raise enough money to give him a free hand for the posters as well as the literary matter, why then, I tell you, this moral food will turn out to be the greatest boom of the generation."

Mr. Cowper moved a little uneasily in his chair.

"Yours, Mr. Bunsome," he said, "is purely the commercial point of view. So far as Mr. Burton and I are concerned, and Mr. Bomford, too, you must please remember that we are profoundly and absolutely convinced of the almost miraculous properties of this preparation. Its romantic history is a thing we have thoroughly attested. Our only fear at the present moment is that too large a quantity of the constituents of the beans which Mr. Burton has handed over to me, may be found to be distilled from Oriental herbs brought by that old student from the East. However, of that in a few days' time we shall of course be able to speak more definitely."

Mr. Bunsome coughed.

"Anyway," he declared, "that isn't my show. My part is to get the particulars of this thing into shape, draft a prospectus, and engage Rentoul if we can raise the money. I presume Mr. Burton will have no objection to our using his photograph on the posters?"

Burton shivered.

"You must not think of such a thing!" he said, harshly.

Mr. Bunsome was disappointed.

"A picture of yourself as you were as an auctioneer's clerk," he remarked, thoughtfully,—"a little gay in the costume, perhaps, rakish-looking hat and tie, you know, and that sort of thing, leaning over the bar, say, of a public-house—and a picture of yourself as you are now, writing in a library one of those little articles of yours—the two together, now, one each side, would have a distinct and convincing effect."

Burton rose abruptly to his feet.

"These details," he said, "I must leave to Mr. Cowper. You have the beans. I have done my share."

The professor caught hold of his arm.

"Sit down, my dear fellow—sit down," he begged. "We have not finished our discussion. The whole subject is most engrossing. We cannot have you hurrying away. Mr. Bunsome's suggestion is, of course, hideously Philistine, but, after all, we want the world to know the truth."

"But the truth about me," Burton protested, "may not be the truth about this food. How do you know that you can reproduce the beans at all in an artificial manner?"

"Science, my young friend—science," the professor murmured. "I tell you that the problem is already nearly solved."

"Supposing you do solve it," Burton continued, "supposing you do produce a food which will have the same effect as the beans, do you realize what you are doing? You will create a revolution. You will break up life-long friendships, you will revolutionize business, you will swamp the divorce courts, you will destroy the whole fabric of social life for at least a generation. Truth is the most glorious thing which the brain of man ever conceived, but I myself have had some experience of the strange position one occupies who has come under its absolutely compelling influence. The world as it is run to-day could never exist for a week without its leaven of lies."

Mr. Bunsome looked mystified. The professor, however, inclined his head sympathetically.

"It is my intention," he remarked, "in drafting my final prescription, that the action of the food shall not be so violent. If the quantities are less strenuously mixed, the food, as you can surmise, will be so much the milder. A gentle preference for truth, a dawning appreciation of beauty, a gradual withdrawal from the grosser things of life—these may, perhaps, be conceived after a week's trial of the food. Then a regular course of it—say for six months or so—would build up these tendencies till they became a part of character. The change, as you see, would not be too sudden. That is my idea, Bomford. We have not heard much from you this evening. What do you think?"

"I agree with you entirely, professor," Mr. Bomford pronounced. "For many reasons it will be as well, I think, to render the food a little less violent in its effects."

Mr. Bunsome began to chuckle to himself. An imperfectly developed sense of humor was asserting itself.

"It's a funny idea!" he exclaimed. "The more one thinks of it, the funnier it becomes. Supposing for a moment—you all take it so seriously—supposing for a moment that the food were to turn out to really have in it some of these qualities, what a mess a few days of it would make of the Stock Exchange! It would mean chaos, sir!"

"It is our hope," the professor declared, sternly, "our profound hope, that this enterprise of ours will not only bring great fortunes to ourselves but will result in the moral elevation of the whole world. There are medicines—patent medicines, too—which have cured thousands of bodily diseases. Why should we consider ourselves too sanguine when we hope that ours, the first real attempt to minister to the physical side of morals, may be equally successful?"

Burton stole away. In the garden he found Edith. They sat together upon a seat and she allowed her hand to remain in his.

"I never knew father so wrapped up in anything as he is in this new scheme," she whispered. "He is even worse than Mr. Bomford."

Burton shivered a little as he leaned back and closed his eyes.

"It is a nightmare!" he groaned. "Have you seen all those advertisements of brain foods? The advertisement columns of our magazines and newspapers are full of them. Their announcements grin down upon us from every hoarding. Do you know that we are going to do the same thing? We are going to contribute our share to the defilement of journalism. We are going to make a similar appeal to the quack instincts of the credulous."

She laughed softly at him.

"You foolish person," she murmured. "Father has been talking to me about it for hours at a time. You are taking it for granted that they will not be able to transmit the qualities of the bean into this new food, but father is sure that they will. Supposing they succeed, why should you object? Why should not the whole world share in this thing which has come to you?"

"I do not know," he answered, a little wearily, "and yet nothing seems to be able to alter the way I feel about it. It seems as though we were committing sacrilege. Your father and Mr. Bomford, and now this man Bunsome, are entirely engrossed in the commercial side of it. If it were to be a gift to the world, a real philanthropic enterprise, it would be different."

"The world wasn't made for philanthropists, dear," she reminded him. "We are only poor human beings, and in our days we have to eat and drink and love."

"If only Mr. Bomford—" he began—

She laid her fingers warningly upon his arm. Mr. Bomford was coming across the lawn towards them. "If you go off alone with him," Burton whispered, "I'll get back the beans and swamp the enterprise. I swear it."

"IF YOU LEAVE US ALONE together," she answered softly, "I'll never speak to you again."

She sprang lightly to her feet.

"Come," she declared, "it is chilly out here to-night. We are all going back into the drawing-room. I am going to make you listen while I sing."

Mr. Bomford looked dissatisfied. He was flushed with wine and he spoke a little thickly.

"If I could have five minutes—" he began.

Edith shook her head.

"I am much too cold," she objected. "Besides, I want to hear Mr. Bunsome talk about the new discovery. Have you found a title for the food yet?"

She walked rapidly on with Burton. Mr. Bomford followed them.

"We have decided," he said, "to call it Menatogen."

XXV

Discontent

Burton gave a little start of surprise as he entered Mr. Waddington's office. Seated on the chair usually occupied by clients, was Ellen.

"My dear Burton," Mr. Waddington exclaimed, with an air of some relief, "your arrival is most opportune! Your wife has just paid me a visit. We were discussing your probable whereabouts only a moment ago."

"Rooms all shut up," Ellen declared, "and not a word left behind nor nothing, and little Alfred come down with a messenger boy, in such a mess as never was!"

"I hope he arrived safely?" Burton inquired. "I found it necessary to send him home."

"He arrived all right," Ellen announced.

"You found a change in him?" Burton asked.

"If you mean about his finicking ways, I do find a change," Ellen replied, "and a good job, too. He's playing with the other boys again and using those silly books to shoot at with a catapult, which to my mind is a sight more reasonable than poring over them all the time. I never did see a man," she continued, with a slow smile, "so taken aback as Mr. Denschem, when he came to take him to the museum yesterday. Little Alf wouldn't have nothing to do with him at any price."

Burton sighed.

"I am afraid," he said politely, "that you may have been inconvenienced by not hearing from me on Saturday."

"'Inconvenienced' is a good word," Ellen remarked. "I've managed to pay my way till now, thank you. What I came up to know about is this!" she went on, producing a copy of the Daily Press from her reticule and smoothing it out on her knee.

Burton groaned. He looked anxiously at Mr. Waddington.

"Have you read it, sir?" he asked.

Mr. Waddington shook his head.

"I make it a rule," he said, "to avoid the advertisement columns of all newspapers. These skilfully worded announcements only serve to remind us how a man may prostitute an aptitude, if not an art, for sheer purposes of gain. It is my theory, Mrs. Burton," he went on, addressing her, "that no one has a right to use his peculiar capacities for the production of any sort of work which is in the least unworthy; which does not aim—you follow me, I am sure?—at the ideal."

Ellen stared at him for a moment.

"I don't follow you," she declared, brusquely, "and I don't know as I want to. About that advertisement, is it you, Alfred, who's to be one of the directors of this Menatogen or whatever they call it? Are they your experiences that are given here?"

"They are!" Burton groaned.

Mr. Waddington, with a heavy frown, took the paper.

"What is this, Burton?" he demanded.

"You had better read it," Burton replied, sinking into a chair. "I mentioned it to you a little time ago. You see, the scheme has finally come to fruition."

Mr. Waddington read the advertisement through, word by word. One gathered that the greatest discovery for many thousands of years would shortly be announced to the world. A certified and unfailing tonic for the moral system was shortly to be placed upon the market. A large factory had been engaged for the manufacture of the new commodity, and distributing warehouses in a central neighborhood. First come, first served. Ten and sixpence a jar. The paper fluttered out of Mr. Waddington's fingers. He looked across at Burton. Burton sank forward in his chair, his head fell into his hands.

"What I want to know," Ellen continued, in a tone of some excitement, "is—what is there coming to us for this? I never did give you credit, Alfred—not in these days, at any rate—for so much common sense. I see they have made you a director. If there's anything in those rotten beans of yours, you've more in your head than I thought, to be trying to make a bit of use of them. What are you getting out of it?"

There was a dead silence. Mr. Waddington had the appearance of a man who has received a shock. Burton withdrew his hands from before his face. He was looking pale and miserable.

"I am getting money," he admitted slowly. "I am getting a great deal of money."

Ellen nodded. Her face betokened the liveliest interest. Mr. Waddington sat like a musician listening to an ill-played rendering of his favorite melody. Burton thrust his hand into his pocket.

"I failed to send you your three pounds on Saturday, Ellen," he said. "Here are thirty—three hundred, if you will. Take them and leave me for a little time."

It is not too much to say that Ellen grabbed at the notes. She counted them carefully and thrust them into her reticule. Her manner was indicating a change. The hard contempt had gone from her face. She looked at her husband with something like awe. After all, this was the signal and final proof of greatness—he had made money!

"Aren't you pleased about it?" she asked sharply. "Not that I ever thought you'd have the wits to turn anything like this into real, solid account!"

Burton set his teeth.

"I am afraid," he said, "that I cannot quite explain how I feel about it. There will be plenty of money for you—for some time, at any rate. You can buy the house, if you like, or buy one somewhere else."

"What about you?" she demanded. "Ain't you coming back?"

He did not move. She rose to her feet, raised her veil and came over to where he was sitting. He smelt the familiar odor of "Lily of the Valley" perfume, blended with the odor of cleaned gloves and benzine. The air around him was full of little violet specks from her boa. She laid her hand upon his shoulder.

"Come and be a man again, Alfred," she begged, a little awkwardly. "You've got good common sense at the bottom still, I am sure. Why don't you give up this tomfoolery and come home to me and the boy? Or shall I stay up," she went on, "and have a little evening in town? You've got the money. Why not let's go to a restaurant and a music-hall afterwards? We might ask the Johnsons. Little Alf would be all right, and I put on my best hat, in case."

Burton looked wearily up.

"Ellen," he said, "I am afraid I can't make you understand. It is true that I shall probably be rich, but I hate the thought of it. I only want to be left alone. I have made a mistake, and yet, Heaven knows, it was hard for me to escape! Before very long," he added, his voice sinking a little lower, "it is quite likely that you will recognize me again completely. I dare say then I shall be very glad to go to the theatre with you and to meet the Johnsons. Just now I—I can't."

Ellen began to tremble.

"Before long you'll be very glad, eh?" she exclaimed. "Well, we'll see about that! I'm sick of this begging and praying of you to behave like a reasonable person. If there's another woman who's come along, why, out with it and let me know?"

"You don't understand," Mr. Waddington interrupted, gently. "Your husband and I have both come under the influence of these—these beans. It is not possible for us to live as we have been accustomed to live."

"Well, I like that!" Ellen declared. "Do you mean to say this is going on?"

Burton looked up.

"On the contrary," he announced, "it is coming to an end—with me, at any rate. Until it does come to an end, it will be kinder of you, and better for both of us, for you to keep away."

She stood for a moment quite still. Her back was turned to them, her shoulders were moving. When she spoke, however, her tone was still hard and unsympathetic.

"Very well," she said, "I'll get back to Garden Green. But mind you, my man," she went on, "none of your sneaking back home just when you're ready for it! Next time it shall be as I choose. I'm no wishy-washy creature, to be your wife one moment and something you can't bear even to look at, the next. No, I don't want none of your monkey tricks, opening the door!" she went on angrily, as Burton rose to see her out. "Stay where you are. I can find my way out of the place."

She departed, slamming the door after her. Mr. Waddington came and sat down by his former clerk's side.

"Tell me, Burton," he asked kindly, "how did you come to do this thing?"

"It was the professor and the girl," he murmured. "They made it seem so reasonable."

"It is always the girl," Mr. Waddington reflected. "The girl with the blue eyes, I suppose, whom you told me about? The girl of the garden?"

Burton nodded.

"Her father is a scientific man," he explained. "He wants money badly to go on with some excavations in Assyria. Between them all, I consented. Waddington," he went on, looking up, "I was beginning to get terrified. I had only two beans left. I have parted with them. They could have lasted me only a few months. I thought if I had to go back, I would go back free from any anxieties of work in an office. Wealth must help one somehow. If I can travel, surround myself with books, live in the country, I can't ever be so bad, I can't fall back where I was before.

What do you think, Mr. Waddington? You must have this on your mind sometimes. You yourself have only six or seven months left."

Mr. Waddington sighed.

"Do you think that it isn't a nightmare for me, too?" he said gently. "Only I am afraid that wealth will not help you. The most vulgar and ignorant people I know are among the wealthiest. There is a more genuine simplicity and naturalness among the contented and competent poor than any other class. You were wrong, Burton. Riches breed idleness, riches tempt one to the purchase of false pleasure. You would have been better back upon your stool in my office."

"It is too late," Burton declared, a little doggedly. "I came to ask you if you wanted to join? For two more beans they would make you, too, a director, and give you five thousand shares."

Mr. Waddington shook his head.

"Thank you, Burton," he said, "I would sooner retain my beans. I have no interest in your enterprise. I think it hateful and abominable. I cannot conceive," he went on, "how you, Burton, in your sane mind, could have stooped so low as to associate yourself in any way with the thing."

"You don't know what my temptations were!" Burton groaned.

"And therefore," Mr. Waddington replied, "I will not judge you. Yet do not think that I should ever allow myself to consider your proposition, even for a moment. Tell me, you say you've parted with your last bean—"

"And my time is almost up!" Burton interrupted, beating the table before him. "Only this morning, for an instant, I was afraid!"

"Try and keep your thoughts away from it," Mr. Waddington advised. "Let me show you these new prints. By the bye, where is your wonderful little boy?"

"Gone—back to his mother!" Burton answered grimly. "Didn't you hear us mention him? I left him in my rooms one night and when I came back the whole place was in disorder. He was in a filthy state and sobbing for his home."

"My poor fellow!" Mr. Waddington murmured. "Come, I will take you with me to lunch. We can spend the afternoon in my library. I have some new treasures to show you. We will lose ourselves. For a short time, at least, you shall forget."

XXVI

The End of a Wonderful World

M r. Waddington turned his head away quickly and glanced half guiltily towards his companion. To his amazement, Burton had been gazing in the same direction. Their eyes met. Burton coughed.

"A remarkably fine woman, that," Mr. Waddington declared.

Burton looked at him in astonishment.

"My dear Mr. Waddington!" he exclaimed. "You cannot really think so!"

They both turned their heads once more. The woman in question was standing upon the doorstep of a milliner's shop, waiting for a taxicab. In appearance she was certainly somewhat striking, but her hair was flagrantly dyed, her eyebrows darkened, her costume daring, her type obvious.

"A very fine woman indeed, I call her," Mr. Waddington repeated. "Shouldn't mind taking her to lunch. Good mind to ask her."

Burton hesitated for a moment. Then a curious change came into his own face.

"She is rather fetching," he admitted.

The woman suddenly smiled. Mr. Waddington pulled himself together.

"It serves us right," he said, a little severely, and hastening his companion on. "I was looking at her only as a curiosity."

Burton glanced behind and move on reluctantly.

"I call her jolly good-looking," he declared.

Mr. Waddington pretended not to hear. They turned into Jermyn Street.

"There are some vases here, at this small shop round the corner, which I want you particularly to notice, Burton," he continued. "They are perfect models of old Etruscan ware. Did you ever see a more beautiful curve? Isn't it a dream? One could look at a curve like that and it has something the same effect upon one as a line of poetry or a single exquisite thought."

Burton glanced into the window and looked back again over his shoulder. The lady, however, had disappeared.

"Hm!" he remarked. "Very nice vase. Let's get on to lunch. I'm hungry."

Mr. Waddington stopped short upon the pavement and gripped his companion's arm.

"Burton," he said, a trifle hesitatingly, "you don't think—you don't imagine—"

"Not a bit of it!" Burton interrupted, savagely. "One must be a little human now and then. By Jove, old man, there are some ties, if you like! I always did think a yellow one would suit me."

Mr. Waddington pressed him gently along.

"I am not sure," he muttered, "that we are quite in the mood to buy ties. I want to ask you a question, Burton."

"Go ahead."

"You were telling me about this wonderful scheme of your friend the professor's, to make—Menatogen, I think you said. Did you part with both your beans?"

"Both," Burton replied, almost fiercely. "But I've another fortnight or so yet. It can't come before—it shan't!"

"You expect, I suppose, to make a great deal of money?" Mr. Waddington continued.

"We shall make piles," Burton declared. "I have had a large sum already for the beans. My pockets are full of money. Queer how light-hearted it makes you feel to have plenty of money. It's a dull world, you know, after all, and we are dull fellows. Think what one could do, now, with some of the notes I have in my pocket! Hire a motor-car, go to some bright place like the *Metropole* at Brighton—a bright, cheerful, sociable place, I mean, where people who look interesting aren't above talking to you. And then a little dinner, and perhaps a music-hall afterwards, and some supper, and plenty to eat and drink—"

"Burton!" Mr. Waddington gasped. "Stop! Stop at once!"

"Why the dickens should I stop?" Burton demanded.

Mr. Waddington was looking shocked and pained. "You don't mean to tell me," he exclaimed, "that this is your idea of a good time? That you would go to a hotel like the *Metropole* and mix with the people whom you might meet there, and eat and drink too much, and call it enjoyment? Burton, what has come to you?"

Burton was looking a little sullen.

"It's all very well," he grumbled. "We're too jolly careful of ourselves. We don't get much fun. Here's your poky little restaurant. Let's see what it looks like inside."

They entered, and a *maitre d'hôtel* came hurrying to meet them. Burton, however, shook his head.

"This place is no good, Waddington," he decided. "Only about half-a-dozen stodgy old people here, no music, and nothing to look at. Let's go where there's some life. I'll take you. My lunch. Come along."

Mr. Waddington protested but faintly. He murmured a word of apology to the *maitre d'hôtel*, whom he knew, but Burton had already gone on ahead and was whistling for a taxi. With a groan, Mr. Waddington noticed that his hat had slipped a little on one side. There was a distinct return of his rakish manner.

"The *Milan!* " Burton ordered. "Get along as quick as you can. We are hungry."

The two men sat side by side in the taxicab. Mr. Waddington watched his companion in half-pained eagerness. Burton certainly was looking much more alert than earlier in the morning.

"I tell you money's a great thing," the latter went on, producing a cigarette from his pocket and lighting it. "I don't know why I should have worried about this little business adventure. I call it a first-class idea. I'd like to be able to take taxies whenever I wanted them, and go round to the big restaurants and sit and watch the people. Come to a music-hall one night, Mr. Waddington, won't you? I haven't seen anything really funny for a long time."

"I'm afraid I should like to," Mr. Waddington began,—"I mean I should be delighted."

"What are you afraid about?" Burton asked quickly.

Mr. Waddington mopped his forehead with his handkerchief.

"Burton," he said hoarsely, "I think it's coming on! I'm glad we are going to the *Milan*. I wish we could go to a music-hall to-night. That woman was attractive!"

Burton set his teeth.

"I can't help it," he muttered. "I can't help anything. Here goes for a good time!"

He dismissed the taxi and entered the Milan, swaggering just a little. They lunched together and neither showed their usual discrimination in the selection of the meal. In place of the light wine which Mr. Waddington generally chose, they had champagne. They drank Benedictine with their coffee and smoked cigars instead of cigarettes. Their conversation was a trifle jerky and Mr. Waddington kept on returning to the subject of the Menatogen Company.

"You know, I've three beans left, Burton," he explained, towards the end of the meal. "I don't know why I should keep them. They'd only last a matter of seven months, anyway. I've got to go back sometime. Do you think I could get in with you in the company?"

"We'll go and—Why, there is Mr. Bunsome!" Burton exclaimed. "Mr. Bunsome!"

The company promoter was just passing their table. He turned around at the sound of his name. For a moment he failed to recognize Burton. There was very little likeness between the pale, contemptuous young man with the dreamy eyes, who had sat opposite to him at the professor's dinner table a few nights ago, and this flushed young man who had just attracted his attention, and who had evidently been lunching exceedingly well. It was part of his business, however, to remember faces, and his natural aptitude came to his assistance.

"How do you do, Mr. Burton?" he said. "Glad to meet you again. Spending some of the Menatogen profits, eh?"

"Friend of mine here—Mr. Waddington," Burton explained. "Mr. Cowper knows all about him. He owns the rest of the beans, you know."

Mr. Bunsome was at once interested.

"I'm delighted to meet you, Mr. Waddington!" he declared, holding out his hand. "Indirectly, you are connected with one of the most marvelous discoveries of modern days."

"I should like to make it 'directly,'" Mr. Waddington said. "Do you think my three beans would get me in on the ground floor?"

Mr. Bunsome was a little surprised.

"I understood from the professor," he remarked, "that your friend was not likely to care about entering into this?"

Burton, for a moment, half closed his eyes.

"I remember," he said. "Last night I didn't think he would care about it. I find I was mistaken."

Mr. Bunsome looked at his watch.

"I am meeting Mr. Cowper this afternoon," he said, "and Mr. Bomford. I know that the greatest difficulty that we have to face at present is the very minute specimens of this wonderful—er—vegetable, from which we have to prepare the food. I should think it very likely that we might be able to offer you an interest in return for your beans. Will you call at my office, Mr. Waddington, at ten o'clock to-morrow morning—number 17, Norfolk Street?"

"With pleasure," Mr. Waddington assented. "Have a drink?"

Mr. Bunsome did not hesitate—it was not his custom to refuse any offer of the sort! He sat down at their table and ordered a sherry and bitters. Mr. Waddington seemed to have expanded. He did not mention the subject of architecture. More than once Mr. Bunsome glanced with some surprise at Burton. The young man completely puzzled him. They talked about Menatogen and its possibilities, and Burton kept harking back to the subject of profits. Mr. Bunsome at last could contain his curiosity no longer.

"Say," he remarked, "you had a headache or something the other night, I think? Seemed as quiet as they make 'em down at the old professor's. I tell you I shouldn't have known you again."

Burton was suddenly white. Mr. Waddington plunged in.

"Dry old stick, the professor, anyway, from what I've heard," he said. "Now don't you forget, Mr. Bunsome. I shall be round at your office at ten o'clock sharp to-morrow, and I expect to be let into the company. Three beans I've got, and remember they're worth something. They took that old Egyptian Johnny—him and his family, of course—a matter of a thousand years to grow, and there's no one else on to them. Why, they're unique, and they do the trick, too—that I can speak for. Paid the bill, Burton?"

Burton nodded. The two men shook hands with Mr. Bunsome and prepared to leave. They walked out into the Strand.

"Got anything to do this afternoon particular?" Mr. Waddington asked, after a moment's hesitation.

"Not a thing," Burton replied, puffing at his cigar and unconsciously altering slightly the angle of his hat.

"Wouldn't care about a game of billiards at the Golden Lion, I suppose?" Mr. Waddington suggested.

"Rather!" Burton assented. "Let's buy the girls some flowers and take a taxi down. Go down in style, eh? I'll pay."

Mr. Waddington looked at his companion—watched him, indeed, hail the taxi—and groaned. A sudden wave of half-ashamed regret swept through him. It was gone, then, this brief peep into a wonderful world! His own fall was imminent. The click of the balls was in his ears, the taste of strong drink was inviting him. The hard laugh and playful familiarities of the buxom young lady were calling to him. He sighed and took his place by his companion's side.

XXVII

Mr. Waddington Also

With his hat at a very distinct angle indeed, with a fourpenny cigar, ornamented by a gold band, in his mouth, Burton sat before a hard-toned piano and vamped.

"Pretty music, The Chocolate Soldier," he remarked, with an air of complete satisfaction in his performance.

Miss Maud, who was standing by his side with her hand laid lightly upon his shoulder, assented vigorously.

"And you do play it so nicely, Mr. Burton," she said. "It makes me long to see it again. I haven't been to the theatre for heaven knows how long!"

Burton turned round in his stool. "What are you doing to-night?" he asked. "Nothing," the young lady replied, eagerly. "Take me to the theatre, there's a dear."

"Righto!" he declared. "I expect I can manage it."

Miss Maud waltzed playfully around the room, her hands above her head. She put her head out of the door and called into the bar.

"Milly, Mr. Burton's taking me to the theatre to-night. Why don't you get Mr. Waddington to come along? We can both get a night off if you make up to the governor for a bit."

"I'll try," was the eager reply,—"that is, if Mr. Waddington's agreeable."

Maud came back to her place by the piano. She was a plump young lady with a pink and white complexion, which suffered slightly from lack of exercise and fresh air and over-use of powder. Her hair was yellower than her friend's, but it also owed some part of its beauty to artificial means. In business hours she was attired in an exceedingly tight-fitting black dress, disfigured in many places by the accidents of her profession.

"You are a dear, Mr. Burton," she declared. "I wonder what your wife would say, though?" she added, a little coyly.

"Not seeing much of Ellen just lately," Burton replied. "I'm living up in town alone."

"Oh!" she remarked. "Mr. Burton, I'm ashamed of you! What does that mean, I wonder? You men!" she went on, with a sigh. "One has to be so careful. You are such deceivers, you know! What's the attraction?"

"You!" he whispered.

"What a caution you are!" she exclaimed. "I like that, too, after not coming near me for months! What are you looking so scared about, all of a sudden?"

Burton was looking through the garishly papered walls of the public-house sitting-room, out into the world. He was certainly a little paler.

"Haven't I been in for months?" he asked softly.

She stared at him.

"Well, I suppose you know!" she retorted. "Pretty shabby I thought it of you, too, after coming in and making such a fuss as you used to pretty well every afternoon. I don't like friends that treat you like that. Makes you careful when they come round again. I'd like to know what you've been doing?"

"Ah!" he said, "you will never know that. Perhaps I myself shall never know that really again. Get me a whiskey and soda, Maud. I want a drink."

"I should say you did!" the young woman declared, pertly. "Sitting there, looking struck all of a heap! Some woman, I expect, you've been gone on. You men are all the same. I've no patience with you—not a bit. If it wasn't," she added, taking down the whiskey bottle from the shelf, "that life's so precious dull without you, I wouldn't have a thing to say to you—no, not me nor Milly either! We were both talking about you and Mr. Waddington only a few nights ago, and of the two I'm not sure that he's not the worst. A man at his age ought to know his mind. Special Scotch—there you are, Mr. Burton. Hope it will do you good."

Burton drank his whiskey and soda as though he needed it. He was suddenly pale, and his fingers were idle upon the keys of the pianoforte. The girl looked at him curiously.

"Not quite yourself, are you?" she inquired. "Don't get chippy before this evening. I don't think I'll give you anything else to drink. When a gentleman takes me out, I like him to be at his best."

Burton came back. It was a long journey from the little corner of the world into which his thoughts had strayed, to the ornate, artificial-looking parlor, with the Turkey-carpet upon the floor and framed advertisements upon the walls.

"I am sorry," he said. "I had forgotten. I can't take you out to-night— I've got an engagement. How I shall keep it I don't know," he went on, half reminiscently, "but I've got to."

The young woman looked at him with rising color. "Well, I declare!" she exclaimed. "You're a nice one, you are! You come in for the first time for Lord knows how long, you agree to take me out this evening, and then, all of a sudden, back out of it! I've had enough of you, Mr. Burton. You can hook it as soon as you like."

Burton rose slowly to his feet.

"I am sorry," he said simply. "I suppose I am not quite myself to-day. I was just thinking how jolly it would be to take you out and have a little supper afterwards, when I remembered—I remembered—that engagement. I've got to go through with it."

"Another girl, I suppose?" she demanded, turning away to look at herself in the mirror.

He shivered. He was in a curious state of mind but there seemed to him something heretical in placing Edith among the same sex.

"It is an engagement I can't very well break," he confessed. "I'll come in again."

"You needn't," she declared, curtly. "When I say a thing, I mean it. I've done with you."

Burton crossed the threshold into the smaller room, where Mr. Waddington appeared to be deriving a certain amount of beatific satisfaction from sitting in an easy-chair and having his hand held by Miss Milly. They both looked at him, as he entered, in some surprise.

"What have you two been going on about?" the young lady asked. "I heard Maud speaking up at you. Some lovers' quarrel, I suppose?"

The moment was passing. Burton laughed—a little hardly, perhaps, but boisterously.

"Maud's mad with me," he explained. "I thought I could take her out to-night. Remembered afterwards I couldn't. Say, old man, you're going it a bit, aren't you?" he continued, shaking his head at his late employer.

Mr. Waddington held his companion's hand more tenderly than ever.

"At your age," he remarked, severely, "you shouldn't notice such things. Milly and I are old friends, aren't we?" he added, drawing her to him.

"Well, it's taken a bit of making up my mind to forgive you," the young lady admitted. "What a pity you can't bring Maud along to-night!" she went on, addressing Burton. "We're going to Frascati's to dinner and into the Oxford afterwards. Get along back and make it up with her. You can easily break your other engagement."

Burton swaggered back to the threshold of the other room.

"Hi! Come along, Maudie!" he said. "I can't take you out to-night but I'll take you to-morrow night, and I'll stand a bottle of champagne now to make up for it."

"Don't want your champagne," the young lady began;—"leastways," she added, remembering that, after all, business was supposed to be her first concern, "I won't say 'no' to a glass of wine with you, but you mustn't take it that you can come in here and do just as you please. I may go out with you some other evening, and I may not. I don't think I shall. To-night just happens to suit me."

With a last admiring glance at herself in the mirror, she came into the room. Burton patted her on the arm and waved the wine list away.

"The best is good enough," he declared,—"the best in the house. Just what you like yourself. Price don't matter just now."

He counted a roll of notes which he drew from his trousers pocket. The two girls looked at him in amazement. He threw one upon the table.

"Backed a horse?" Maud asked. "Legacy?" Milly inquired. Burton, with some difficulty, relit the stump of his cigar.

"Bit of an advance I've just received from a company I'm connected with," he explained. "Would insist on my being a director. I'm trying to get Waddington here into it," he added, condescendingly. "Jolly good thing for him if I succeed, I can tell you."

Miss Maud moved away in a chastened manner. She took the opportunity to slip upstairs and powder her face and put on clean white cuffs. Presently she returned, carrying the wine on a silver tray, with the best glasses that could be procured.

"Here's luck!" Burton exclaimed, jauntily. "Can't drink much myself. This bubbly stuff never did agree with me and I had a good go at it last night."

Maud filled up his glass, nevertheless, touched it with her own, and drank, looking at him all the time with an expression in her eyes upon which she was wont to rely.

"Take me out to-night, dear," she whispered. "I feel just like having a good time to-night. Do!"

Burton suddenly threw his glass upon the floor. The wine ran across the carpet in a little stream. Splinters of the glass lay about in all directions. They all three looked at him, transfixed.

"I am sorry," he said.

He turned and walked out of the room. They were all too astonished to stop him. They heard him cross the bar-room and they heard the door close as he passed into the street.

"Of all the extraordinary things!" Maud declared.

"Well, I never!" Milly gasped.

"If Mr. Burton calls that behaving like a gentleman—" Maud continued, in a heated manner—Mr. Waddington patted her on the shoulder.

"Hush, hush, my dear!" he said. "Between ourselves, Burton has been going it a bit lately. There's no doubt that he's had a drop too much to drink this afternoon. Don't take any notice of him. He'll come round all right. I can understand what's the matter with him. You mark my words, in two or three days he'll be just his old self."

"Has he come into a fortune, or what?" Maud demanded. "He's left you, hasn't he?"

Mr. Waddington nodded.

"He's found a better job," he admitted. "Kind of queer in his health, though. I've been taken a little like it myself, but those sort of things pass off—they pass off."

Milly looked at him curiously. He was suddenly quiet.

"Why, you're looking just like Mr. Burton did a few minutes ago!" she declared. "What's the matter with you? Can you see ghosts?" Mr. Waddington sat quite still. "Yes," he muttered, "I see ghosts!"

They looked at him in a puzzled manner. Then Milly leaned towards him and filled his glass with Wine. She touched his glass with her own, she even suffered her arm to rest upon his shoulder. For a single moment Mr. Waddington appeared to feel some instinct of aversion. He seemed almost about to draw away. Then the mood passed. He drew her towards him with a little burst of laughter, and raised his glass to his lips.

"Here's fun!" he exclaimed. "Poor old Burton!"

XXVIII

THE REAL ALFRED BURTON

E dith slipped out of her evening cloak and came into the foyer of the Opera House, a spotless vision of white. For a moment she looked at her cavalier in something like amazement. It did not need the red handkerchief, a corner of which was creeping out from behind his waistcoat, to convince her that some extraordinary change had taken place in Burton. He was looking pale and confused, and his quiet naturalness of manner had altogether disappeared. He came towards her awkwardly, swinging a pair of white kid gloves in his hand.

"Bit late, aren't you?" he remarked.

"I am afraid I am a few minutes late," she admitted. "Until the last moment father said he was coming. We shall have to go in very quietly."

"Come along, then," he said. "I don't know the way. I suppose one of these fellows will tell us."

His inquiry, loud-voiced and not entirely coherent, received at first scant attention from the usher to whom he addressed himself. They were directed to their places at last, however. The house was in darkness, and with the music Edith forgot, for a time, the slight shock which she had received. The opera was Samson et Dalila, and a very famous tenor was making his reappearance after a long absence. Edith gave herself up to complete enjoyment of the music. Then suddenly she was startled by a yawn at her side. Burton was sitting back, his hands in his pockets, his mouth wide-open.

"Mr. Burton!" she exclaimed softly. He had the grace to sit up. "Long-winded sort of stuff, this," he pronounced, in an audible whisper.

She felt a cold shiver of apprehension. As she saw him lounging there beside her, her thoughts seemed to go back to the day when she had looked with scornful disdain at that miserable picnic-party of trippers, who drank beer out of stone jugs, and formed a blot upon the landscape. Once more she saw the man who stood a little apart, in his loud clothes and common cloth cap, saw him looking into the garden. She began to tremble. What had she done—so nearly done! In spite of herself, the music drew her away again. She even found herself turning towards him once for sympathy.

"Isn't it exquisite?" she murmured.

He laughed shortly.

"Give me The Chocolate Soldier," he declared. "Worth a dozen of this!"

Suddenly she realized what had happened. Her anger and resentment faded away. For the first time she wholly and entirely believed his story. For the first time she felt that this miracle had come to pass. She was no longer ashamed of him. She no longer harbored any small feelings of resentment at his ill-bred attitude. A profound sympathy swept up from her heart—sympathy for him, sympathy, too, for herself. When they passed out together she was as sweet to him as possible, though he put on a black bowler hat some time before it was necessary, and though his red handkerchief became very much in evidence.

"You will drive me down to Chelsea, won't you?" she begged.

"Righto!" he replied. "I'll get one of these chaps to fetch a taxi."

He succeeded in obtaining one, gleeful because he had outwitted some prior applicant to whom the cab properly belonged.

"Couldn't stop somewhere and have a little supper, could we?" he asked.

"I am afraid not," she answered. "It wouldn't be quite the thing."

He tried to take her hand. After a moment's hesitation she permitted it.

"Mr. Burton," she said softly, "do answer me one question. Did you part with all your beans?"

His hand went up to his forehead for a moment.

"Yes," he replied, "both of them. I only had two, and it didn't seem worth while keeping one. Got my pockets full of money, too, and they are going to make me a director of Menatogen."

"Do you feel any different?" she asked him.

He looked at her in a puzzled way and, striking a match, lit a cigarette without her permission.

"Odd you should ask that," he remarked. "I do feel sort of queer to-night—as though I'd been ill, or something of the sort. There are so many things I can only half remember—at least I remember the things themselves, but the part I took in them seems so odd. Kind of feeling as though I'd been masquerading in another chap's clothes," he added, with an uneasy little laugh. "I don't half like it."

"Tell me," she persisted, "did you really find the music tiresome?"

E. PHILLIPS OPPENHEIM

He nodded.

"Rather," he confessed. "The Chocolate Soldier is my idea of music. I like something with a tune in it. There's been no one to beat Gilbert and Sullivan. I don't know who wrote this Samson and Delilah, but he was a dismal sort of beggar, wasn't he? I like something cheerful. Don't you want to come and have some supper, Edith? I know a place where they play all the popular music."

"No, thank you," she told him gravely.

"You seem so cold and sort of stand-offish to-night," he complained, coming a little closer to her. "Some of those nights down at your place—can't remember 'em very well but I am jolly sure you were different. What's happened? Mayn't I hold your fingers, even?"

His arm would have been around her waist, but she evaded it firmly.

"Don't you know what has happened?" she demanded, earnestly. "Don't you really know?"

"Can't say that I do," he admitted. "I've got a sort of feeling as though I'd been all tied-up like, lately. Haven't been able to enjoy myself properly, and gone mooning about after shadows. To-night I feel just as though I were coming into my own again a bit. I say," he added, admiringly, "you do look stunning! Come and have some supper—no one will know—and let me drive you home afterwards. Do!"

She shook her head.

"I don't think you must talk to me quite like this," she said kindly. "You have a wife, you know, and I am engaged to be married."

He laughed, quite easily.

"Never seen Ellen, have you?" he remarked. "She's a fine woman, you know, although she isn't quite your style. She'd think you sort of pale and colorless, I expect—no kind of go or dash about you."

"Is that what you think?" Edith asked him, smiling.

"You aren't exactly the style I've always admired," he confessed, "but there's something about you," he added, in a puzzled manner,—"I don't know what it is but I remember it from a year ago—something that seemed to catch hold of me. I expect I must be a sentimental sort of Johnny underneath. However, I do admire you, Edith, immensely. I only wish—"

Again she evaded him.

"Please do not forget Mr. Bomford," she begged.

"That silly old ass!" Burton exclaimed. "Looks as though he'd swallowed a poker! You're never going to marry him!"

"I think that I shall," she replied. "At any rate, at present I am engaged to him. Therefore, if you please, you must keep just a little further away. I don't like to mention it, but I think—haven't you been smoking rather too much?"

He laughed, without a trace of sensitiveness. "I have been having rather a day of it," he admitted. "But I say, Edith, if you won't come to supper, I think you might let a fellow—"

She drew back into her corner.

"Mr. Burton," she said, "you must please not come near me."

"But I want a kiss," he protested. "You'd have given me one the other night. You'd have given me as many as I'd liked. You almost clung to me—that night under the cedar tree."

Her eyes for a moment were half closed.

"It was a different world then," she whispered softly. "It was a different Mr. Burton. You see, since then a curtain has come down. We are starting a fresh act and I don't think I know you quite so well as I did."

"Sounds like tommyrot," he grumbled.

The taxicab came to a standstill. The man got down and opened the door. Burton half sulkily stepped out on to the pavement.

"Well, here you are," he announced. "Can't say that I think much of you this evening."

She held out her hand. They were standing on the pavement now, in the light of a gas-lamp, and with the chauffeur close at hand. She was not in the least afraid but there was a lump in her throat. He looked so very common, so far away from those little memories with which she must grapple!

"Mr. Burton," she said, "good-night! I want to thank you for this evening and I want to ask you to promise that if ever you are sorry because I persuaded you to sell those little beans, you will forgive me. It was a very wonderful thing, you know, and I didn't understand. Perhaps I was wrong."

"Don't you worry," he answered, cheerfully. "That's all right, anyway. It's jolly well the best thing I ever did in my life. Got my pockets full of money already, and I mean to have a thundering good time with it. No fear of my ever blaming you. Good-night, Miss Edith! My regards to the governor and tell him I am all on for Menatogen."

He gave his hat a little twist and stepped back into the taxi.

"I will give my father your message," she told him, as the door opened to receive her.

"Righto!" Burton replied. "Leicester Square, cabby!"

XXIX

RICHES AND REPENTANCE

There was considerable excitement in Laurence Avenue when a few mornings later Mr. Alfred Burton, in a perfectly appointed motor-car, drew up before the door of Clematis Villa. In a very leisurely manner he descended and stood looking around him for a moment in the front garden.

"Poky little place," he said half to himself, having completed a disparaging survey. "Hullo, Johnson! How are you?"

Mr. Johnson, who, with a little bag in his hand, had just trudged a mile to save a penny, looked with something like amazement at the apparition which confronted him. Mr. Alfred Burton was arrayed in town clothes of the most pronounced cut. His tail coat was exactly the right length; his trousers, although the pattern was a little loud, were exceedingly well cut. He wore patent boots with white gaiters, a carefully brushed silk hat, and he carried in his hand a pair of yellow kid gloves. He had a malacca cane with a gold top under his arm, and a cigar at the usual angle in the corner of his mouth. No wonder that Mr. Johnson, who was, it must be confessed, exceedingly shabby, took his pipe from his mouth and stared at his quondam friend in amazement.

"Hullo, Burton, you back again?" he exclaimed weakly.

"I am back again just to settle up here," Mr. Burton explained, with a wave of the hand. "Just run down in the car to take the missis out a little way."

Mr. Johnson held on to the railing tightly.

"Your car?"

"My car," Mr. Burton admitted, modestly. "Take you for a ride some day, if you like. How's the wife?"

"First-class, thanks," Mr. Johnson replied. "First-class, thank you, Mr. Burton."

Burton protested mildly.

"No need to 'Mr. Burton' me, Johnson, old fellow! It shall never be said of me that a great and wonderful rise in the world altered my feelings towards those with whom I was once on terms of intimacy.

I shall always be glad to know you, Johnson. Thursday evening, isn't it? What are you and the wife doing?"

"I don't know," Johnson confessed, "that we are doing anything particular. We shall turn up at the band, I suppose."

"Good!" Mr. Burton said. "It will be our last Thursday evening in these parts, I expect, but after I have taken the wife for a little spin we'll walk round the band-stand ourselves. Perhaps we shall be able to induce you and Mrs. Johnson to come back and take a little supper with us?"

Mr. Johnson pulled himself together.

"Very kind of you, old cocky," he declared, tremulously. "Been striking it thick, haven't you?"

Burton nodded.

"Dropped across a little thing in the city," he remarked, flicking the dust from the sleeve of his coat. "Jolly good spec it turned out. They made me a director. It's this new Menatogen Company. Heard of it?"

"God bless my soul, of course I have!" Johnson exclaimed. "Millions in it, they say. The shares went from par to four premium in half an hour. I know a man who had a call of a hundred. He's cleared four hundred pounds."

Mr. Burton nodded in a most condescending manner.

"That so?" he remarked. "I've a matter of ten thousand myself, besides some further calls, but I'm not selling just yet. If your friend's got any left, you can tell him from me—and I ought to know as I'm a director—that the shares will be at nine before long. Shouldn't wonder if they didn't go to twenty. It's a grand invention. Best thing I ever touched in my life."

Johnson had been finding it chilly a short time ago but he took off his hat now and mopped his forehead.

"Haven't been home lately, have you?" he remarked.

"To tell you the truth," Mr. Burton explained, puffing at his cigar, "this little affair has been taking up every minute of my time. I had to take chambers in town to keep up with my work. Well, so long, Johnson! See you later at the band-stand. Don't forget we shall be expecting you this evening. May run you up to the west-end, perhaps, if the missis feels like it."

He nodded and proceeded on his way to the front door of his domicile. Mr. Johnson, narrowly escaping an impulse to take off his hat, proceeded on his homeward way.

"Any one at home?" Mr. Burton inquired, letting himself in.

There was no reply. Mr. Burton knocked with his gold-headed cane upon the side of the wall. The door at the end of the passage opened abruptly. Ellen appeared.

"What are you doing there, knocking all the plaster down?" she demanded, sharply. "If you want to come in, why can't you ring the bell? Standing there with your hat on as though the place belonged to you!"

Burton was a little taken aback. He recovered himself, however, secure in the splendid consciousness of his irreproachable clothes and the waiting motor-car. He threw open the door of the parlor.

"Step this way a moment, Ellen," he said. She followed him reluctantly into the room. He put his hand upon her shoulder to lead her to the window. She shook herself free at once.

"Hands off!" she ordered. "What is it you want?"

He pointed out of the window to the magnificent memorial of his success. She looked at it disparagingly.

"What's that? Your taxicab?" she asked. "What did you keep him for? You can get another one at the corner."

Burton gasped.

"Taxicab!" he exclaimed. "Taxicab, indeed! Look at it again. That's a motor-car—my own motor-car. Do you hear that? Bought and paid for!"

"Well, run away and play with it, then!" she retorted, turning as though to leave the room. "I don't want you fooling about here. I'm just getting Alfred's supper." Burton dropped his cigar upon the carpet. Even when he had picked it up, he stood looking at her with his mouth a little open.

"You don't seem to understand, Ellen," he said. "Listen. I've come back home. A share of that motor-car is yours."

"Come back home," Ellen repeated slowly.

"Exactly," he admitted, complacently. "I am afraid this is rather a shock for you, but good news never kills, you know. We'll motor up to the band presently and I've asked the Johnsons to supper. If you've nothing in the house, we'll all go up to the west-end somewhere. . . What's the matter with you?"

Ellen was looking at that moment positively handsome. Her cheeks were scarlet and her eyes ablaze.

"Alfred Burton," she declared, "the last few times I've seen you, I've put you down as being dotty. Now I am sure of it. The sooner you're out of this, the better, before I lose my temper."

"But, my dear Ellen," he protested, soothingly, "I can assure you that what I am telling you is the truth! I have become unexpectedly rich. A fortunate stroke of business—the Menatogen Company, you know—has completely altered our lives. You are naturally overcome—"

"Naturally over-fiddlesticks!" Ellen interrupted. "Look here, my man, I've had about enough of this. You come down here, thinking because you've come to your senses, and because you've got new clothes and a motor-car, that you can just sit down as though nothing had happened. Just let me tell you this—you can't do it! You can leave your wife because she can't stop you. You can stay away from her because she can't drag you back. But you can't come and put on a new suit of clothes and bring a motor-car and say 'I've come back,' and sit down at your usual place and find everything just as you've left it. You can't do that, Alfred Burton, and you must be a bigger fool even than you look to imagine that you can!"

"Ellen," he faltered, "don't you want me back?"

"Not I!" she replied, fiercely. "Not you nor your motor-car nor your money nor any part of you. Come swaggering in, dropping your cigar ash over the place, and behaving as though you'd been a respectable person all your life!" she continued, indignantly. "What right have you got to think that your wife was made to be your slave or your trained dog, to beg when you hold out a piece of biscuit, and go and lie down alone when you don't want her. Send your three pounds a week and get out of it. That's all I want to hear of you! You know the way, don't you?"

Her outstretched forefinger pointed to the door. Burton had never felt so pitifully short of words in his life.

"I—I've asked the Johnsons to supper," he stammered, as he took up his hat.

"Take them to your west-end, then!" Ellen cried, scornfully. "Take them riding in your motor-car. Why don't you tell the man to drive up and down the avenue, that every one may see how fine you are! Would you like to know just what I think of you?"

Burton looked into her face and felt a singular reluctance to listen to the torrent of words which he felt was ready to break upon his head. He tried to hold himself a little more upright.

"You will be sorry for this, Ellen," he said, with some attempt at dignity.

She laughed scornfully.

"One isn't sorry at getting rid of such as you," she answered, and slammed the door behind him.

Burton walked with hesitating footsteps down the footpath. This was not in the least the triumphal return he had intended to make! He stood for a moment upon the pavement, considering. It was curious, but his motor-car no longer seemed to him a glorious vehicle. He was distinctly dissatisfied with the cut of his clothes, the glossiness of his silk hat, his general appearance. The thought of his bank balance failed to bring him any satisfaction whatever. He seemed suddenly, as clearly as though he were looking into a mirror, to see himself with eyes. He recognized even the blatant stupidity of his return, and he admired Ellen more than he had ever admired her in his life.

"Where to, sir?" his brand-new chauffeur asked.

Burton pitched away his cigar.

"Wait a moment," he said, and turning round, walked with firm footsteps back to the house. He tried the door and opened it, looked into the parlor and found it empty. He walked down the passage and pushed open the door of the kitchen. Little Alfred's meal was ready on a tray, the room was spotless and shining, but Ellen, with her head buried in her hands, was leaning forward in her chair, sobbing. He suddenly fell on his knees by her side.

"Please forgive me, Ellen!" he cried, almost sobbing himself. "Please forgive me for being such a rotter. I'll never—I promise that I'll never do anything of the sort again."

She looked up. He ventured to put his arm around her waist. She shook herself free, very weakly. He tried again and with success.

"I know I've made an idiot of myself," he went on. "I'd no right to come down here like that. I just want you to forgive me now, that's all. I didn't mean to swagger about being rich. I'm not enjoying it a bit till you come along."

Ellen raised her head once more. Her lips were' quivering, half with a smile, although the tears were still in her eyes.

"Sure you mean it?" she asked softly.

"Absolutely!" he insisted. "Go and put on your hat with the feathers and we'll meet the Johnsons and take them for a ride."

"You don't like the one with the feathers," she said, doubtfully.

"I like it now," he assured her heartily. "I'm fonder of you at this moment, Ellen, than any one in the world. I always have been, really."

"Stupid!" she declared. "I shall wear my hat with the wing and we will call around at Saunders' and I can buy a motor veil. I always did think that a motor veil would suit me. We'd better call at Mrs. Cross's, too, and have her come in and cook the supper. Don't get into mischief while I'm upstairs."

"I'll come, too—and see little Alfred," he added, hastily.

"Carry the tray, then, and mind where you're going," Ellen ordered.

XXX

A Man's Soul

The half-yearly directors' meeting of the Menatogen Company had just been held. One by one, those who had attended it were taking their leave. The auditor, with a bundle of papers under his arm, shook hands cordially with the chairman—Alfred Burton, Esquire—and Mr. Waddington, and Mr. Bomford, who, during the absence of the professor in Assyria, represented the financial interests of the company.

"A most wonderful report, gentlemen," the auditor pronounced,—"a business, I should consider, without its equal in the world."

"And still developing," Mr. Waddington remarked, impressively.

"And still developing," the auditor agreed. "Another three years like the last and I shall have the pleasure of numbering at least three millionaires among my acquaintances."

"Shall we—?" Mr. Burton suggested, glancing towards Waddington.

Mr. Waddington nodded, but Mr. Bomford took up his hat. He was dressed in the height of subdued fashion. His clothes and manners would have graced a Cabinet Minister. He had, as a matter of fact, just entered Parliament.

"You will excuse me, gentlemen," he said. "I make it a rule never to take anything at all in the middle of the day."

He took his leave with the auditor.

"Pompous old ass!" Mr. Waddington murmured. "A snob!" Mr. Alfred Burton declared,—"that's what I call him! Got his eye on a place in Society. Saw his name in the paper the other day a guest at Lady Somebody's reception. Here goes, old chap—success to Menatogen!"

Waddington drained his glass.

"They say it's his wife who pushes him on so," he remarked.

Mr. Burton's wine went suddenly flat. He drank it but without enjoyment. Then he rose to his feet.

"Well, so long, Waddington, old chap," he said. "I expect the missis is waiting for me."

Mrs. Burton was certainly waiting for her husband. She was sitting back among the cushions of her Sixty horse-power Daimler, wrapped in a motoring coat of the latest fashion, her somewhat brilliant coloring only partially obscured by the silver-gray veil which drooped from her motor bonnet. Burton took his place beside her almost in silence, and they glided off. She looked at him curiously.

"Meeting go off all right?" she asked, a little sharply.

"Top hole," Mr. Burton replied.

"Then what are you so glum about?" she demanded, suspiciously. "You've got nothing to worry about that I can see."

"Nothing at all," Mr. Burton admitted.

"Very good report of Alfred came second post," Mrs. Burton continued. "They say he'll be fit to enter Harrow next year. And an invitation to dine, too, with Lady Goldstein. We're getting on, Alfred. The only thing now is that country house. I wish we could find something to suit us."

"If we keep on looking," Burton remarked, "we are bound to come across something sooner or later. If not, I must build."

"I'm all for building," Mrs. Burton declared. "I don't care for mouldy old ruins, with ivy and damp places upon the walls. I like something fine and spick and span and handsome, with a tower to it, and a long straight drive that you can see down to the road; plenty of stone work about the windows, and good square rooms. As for the garden, well, let that come. We can plant a lot of small trees about, and lay down a lawn. I don't care about other folks' leavings in houses, and a lot of trees around a place always did put me off. Have you told him where to go to?"

Burton shook his head.

"I just told him to drive about thirty or forty miles into the country," he said. "It doesn't matter in what direction, does it? We may see something that will suit us."

The car, with its splendid easy motion, sped noiselessly through the suburbs and out into the country. It seemed to Mr. Burton that he must have dozed. He had been up late the night before, and for several nights before that. He was a little puffy about the cheeks and his eyes were not so bright as they had been. He had developed a habit of dozing off in odd places. When he awoke, he sat up with a start. He had been dreaming. Surely this was a part of the dream! The car was going very slowly indeed. On one side of him was a common, with bushes of flaming gorse and clumps of heather, and little ragged plantations of pine trees; and on his right, a low, old-fashioned house, a lawn of velvet, and a great cedar tree; a walled garden with straight, box-bordered paths, a garden full of old-fashioned flowers whose perfume seemed suddenly to be tearing at some newly-awakened part of the man. He sat up. He stared at the little seat among the rose bushes. Surely he was back again, back again in that strange world, where the flavor of existence was a different thing, where his head had touched the clouds, where all the gross cares and pleasures of his everyday life had fallen away! Was it the perfume of the roses, of the stocks, which had suddenly appealed to some dormant sense of beauty? Or had he indeed passed back for a moment into that world concerning which he had sometimes strange, half doubtful thoughts? He leaned forward, and his eyes wandered feverishly among the hidden places of the garden. The seat was empty. Propped up against the hedge was a notice board: "This House to Let."

"What on earth are you staring at?" Mrs. Burton demanded, with some acerbity. "A silly little place like that would be no use to us. I don't know what the people who've been living there could have been thinking about, to let the garden get into such a state. Fancy a nasty dark tree like that, too, keeping all the sun away from the house! I'd have it cut down if it were mine. What on earth are you looking at, Alfred Burton?"

He turned towards her, heavy-eyed.

"Somewhere under that cedar tree," he said, "a man's soul was buried. I was wondering if its ghost ever walked!"

Mrs. Burton lifted the speaking-tube to her lips.

"You can take the next turning home, John," she ordered.

The man's hand was mechanically raised to his hat. Mrs. Burton leaned back once more among the cushions.

"You and your ghosts!" she exclaimed. "If you want to sit there, thinking like an owl, you'd better try and think of some of your funny stories for to-night. You'll have to sit next that stuck-up Mrs. Bomford, and she takes a bit of amusing."

THE END

A Note About the Author

E. Phillips Oppenheim (1866–1946) was a British writer who rose to prominence in the late nineteenth century. He was born in London to a leather merchant and began working at an early age. Oppenheim spent nearly 20 years in the family business, while juggling a freelance writing career. He composed short stories and eventually novels with more than 100 titles to his credit. His first novel, *Expiation* was published in 1886 followed by *The Mystery of Mr. Bernard Brown* (1896) and *The Long Arm of Mannister* (1910). Oppenheim is best known for his signature tales full of action and espionage.

A Note from the Publisher

Spanning many genres, from non-fiction essays to literature classics to children's books and lyric poetry, Mint Edition books showcase the master works of our time in a modern new package. The text is freshly typeset, is clean and easy to read, and features a new note about the author in each volume. Many books also include exclusive new introductory material. Every book boasts a striking new cover, which makes it as appropriate for collecting as it is for gift giving. Mint Edition books are only printed when a reader orders them, so natural resources are not wasted. We're proud that our books are never manufactured in excess and exist only in the exact quantity they need to be read and enjoyed. To learn more and view our library, go to minteditionbooks.com

bookfinity & ◨ MINT EDITIONS

Enjoy more of your favorite classics with Bookfinity,
a new search and discovery experience for readers.
With Bookfinity, you can discover more vintage
literature for your collection, find your Reader Type,
track books you've read or want to read,
and add reviews to your favorite books.
Visit www.bookfinity.com, and click on
Take the Quiz to get started.

Don't forget to follow us
@bookfinityofficial and @mint_editions

CPSIA information can be obtained
at www.ICGtesting.com
Printed in the USA
BVHW041016280322
632627BV00007B/161